Other Five Star Titles
by Wayne D. Overholser:

TWIN ROCKS

TWIN ROCKS
A Western Duo

WAYNE D. OVERHOLSER

Five Star • Waterville, Maine

First Edition
First Printing: August 2005

Published in 2005 in conjunction with
Golden West Literary Agency.

Set in 11 pt. Plantin by Al Chase.

Printed in the United States on permanent paper.

Library of Congress Cataloging-in-Publication Data

Overholser, Wayne D., 1906–
    [Trouble at Gold Plume]
    Twin Rocks : a western duo / by Wayne D. Overholser.—1st ed.
    p. cm.
    ISBN 1-59414-169-X (hc : alk. paper)
    I. Overholser, Wayne D., 1906– Twin Rocks.   II. Title.
PS3529.V33T76 2005
    813′.54—dc22   2005012059

TWIN ROCKS
A Western Duo

Table of Contents

Trouble at Gold Plume

I

It had been a long chase and so far a futile one, but Jim Harrigan had every reason to believe that the end was in sight. He pulled up his gaunted roan saddler atop Star Mountain Pass, his gaze sweeping the new mining camp of Gold Plume that lay below him, squeezed thin by high granite cliffs hugging the creek. Somewhere in that scattering of frame buildings, log cabins, and tents would be Rush Kane, the man Jim had trailed across the Continental Divide from Dodge City.

Answers to Jim's questions in Pueblo told him Kane had been there less than a week before. Rush Kane, gambler, was not one who could easily be mistaken for another. He had crossed Marshal Pass, paused in Gunnison, and gone on to Ouray. Gradually Jim had closed the gap, and now, if his calculations were right, Kane had ridden into Gold Plume last night.

The promise of winter was in the thin air here on the pass, and Jim did not pause long. He turned his roan down the twisting trail that lay like a looped ribbon against the mountainside, passed a slow-moving line of burros carrying coal to the mining camp, and came into the aspens, aflame now with the gold and orange of fall. But the beauty of this wild land held no lure at that moment for Jim Harrigan was thinking of the job that lay before him, and of his own chances that were, at best, slim. Gold Plume was Duke Madden's town, and Madden would give Kane the help he needed.

Then he was down, the trail cutting across an open park toward the camp. Log ranch buildings lay hard against the cliff, and below him a line of haystacks bulked high along the creek. Jim was surprised because the ranch had been hidden

11

from the trail by overhanging rock, but he was more surprised by the drama that was being enacted here. A girl stood facing a half circle of mounted men, a Winchester in her hands, her voice crisp as she said: "The answer's no, Burke."

"You're smart, ma'am," a familiar voice was saying, "smart enough to see the butter on your bread."

"We'll hold the hay," the girl said firmly.

"You'd better take Madden's offer," the man pressed. "Ten dollars a ton is better'n winding up with nothing."

"Dad said you were bad enough to steal anything!" the girl cried.

"He was a little hard on us." The man laughed softly. "We wouldn't steal the hay. We'd just borrow it. No use packing it in when we've got some right under our nose."

"Still playing the old game, ain't you, Boomer?" Jim asked.

The man wheeled, hands dipping for gun butts, and falling away when the girl said flatly: "I'll kill the first man who draws his iron."

A careful alertness came into Boomer Burke's face. He was a wide man with squeezed features that made him look as if the top of his head had been hammered down toward his feet, leaving his chin where it was. Licking his lips, he turned his gaze back to the girl. "You can put your rifle down, ma'am. Jim Harrigan don't need a woman's help."

Jim leaned forward, hands resting before him, a loose lank man who belonged in the saddle. The dark leather-brown of his cheeks and his sun-bleached blue eyes were evidence that he had spent most of his waking hours where the sun and the wind could touch him. He laughed silently now, a kind of mirth that jarred Boomer Burke and made him shift uneasily in his saddle.

"I've met up with Boomer before," Jim said contemptuously. "He won't pull a gun on me. Not when I'm facing him."

Jim's tongue was a knife ripping skin from Burke's body. His men looked at him as if expecting swift and violent action, but the cool courage that it took to face Jim Harrigan wasn't in him. He said mildly: "I don't see your badge, Jim."

"I'm a private citizen, Boomer."

"Then what in hell are you doing here?"

"Looking at the scenery."

Burke's shrill laugh was a strange sound coming from such a bulky-bodied man. "You've got plenty to see around here." He rubbed a pimply nose. "Harrigan, you wouldn't cross the street to see the purtiest sunset this side of hell. Now what are you doing here?"

"I hear Gold Plume's got five thousand men who've showed up in the last six months. Wouldn't be surprising if another rode in."

"That ain't it, neither." Burke wagged his great head. "You wouldn't know a chunk of gold ore if you saw one. Me and Duke get our fun relieving the other fellow of his *dinero*. You get yours playing bloodhound. Who are you after?"

"Maybe you. Maybe Duke." Jim shrugged. "Still working for Duke, are you?"

"Sure. It's Duke's town." Burke motioned to the girl. "Only some don't know it."

"But Duke's got ways of persuading folks. Even pretty girls."

"That's right." Burke's grin was a wicked tightening of lips against yellow teeth. "If you're after me or Duke, you've got a chore."

Jim built a smoke, his mind making a quick study of this development. Rush Kane had worked for Madden in the Montana gold camps when Jim thought Kane was a square shooter. Now Burke would take word to Madden that Jim Harrigan was in camp and Kane would hear. He'd guess why Jim had come, and he'd ride on, or Madden would ride him out until the sign was right for Jim's removal.

"Might be quite a chore at that." Jim thumbed a match into flame and held it to his cigarette. He flipped the charred stick away, his eyes blue slits. "You tell Duke, Boomer. I'll be looking him up pretty soon."

It was a plain raw challenge, and there wasn't an ounce of bluff in Jim Harrigan. Burke, knowing that, said: "I'll tell him. Belle, you'd better think over what I said." He wheeled his horse toward town, gray dust boiling behind him, his men lining out along the trail.

"I'm Jim Harrigan." Jim raised his hat. "Didn't look like they were shoving you around any, but I couldn't keep my nose out of it."

She held out a brown firm hand that was swallowed by his big one. "I'm Belle Calvert. I'm afraid I was in for more shoving around than you figured. It's a good thing for me you stuck your nose into it."

She was small and slim and straight with black hair and black eyes and a determined chin. To Jim Harrigan, with the long ride and lonely campfires behind him, she made a lovely and distracting picture, the fulfillment of an old and cherished dream.

"I'm glad I was some help," he said.

She tried to smile, and he saw she was close to crying. "I guess you're a rip-roarer from Bitter Creek the way Burke rode off."

"I shave with a Bowie knife and I cut my teeth on a stick of Giant powder." He winked. "What was the ruckus about, ma'am?"

"Duke Madden wants my hay for any song he decides to

sing," she said sourly. "Six months ago Rocking C was one of the biggest spreads in the San Juan. Then they made the strike and miners came in like locusts. They've stolen our beef, killed my father, and I can't pay enough to keep hands."

"I've got an idea the tune Duke would sing," Jim said dryly.

"Get down and rest your saddle," Belle invited. "You won't find a bed in town, and you'll be lucky to get a meal."

"Thanks, but I guess I'd better mosey on." He lifted his reins. "If you have any more trouble with Madden or Burke, let me know."

"I will," she promised. "If you can't find accommodations in town, come back."

"Thanks," he said again, and, raising his hat to her, rode away.

It was after noon when Jim rode into Gold Plume. Sunlight was sharp upon the town, and the air, caught between the high cliffs, was still and hot and gray with the dust that was constantly being churned into motion by burros and men. The dirty turbulent creek ran with swift abandon along the east cliff, and between it and the west wall lay the town, two long lines of buildings and tents threaded by the dusty street.

Gold Plume made no pretensions of dignity or permanence. There was no brick, no stone, no paint. It was a town of pine box houses and tents and rectangles of four planks claiming a building site, a circus with 100 side shows. Stores and offices with canvas tops. Log foundations. Houses with Leadville fronts. Plank walks or dusty paths piled with lumber. Canned goods. Kegs of beer. Here in Gold Plume 1,000 men preyed upon another 1,000 who blasted gold from a stubborn earth. Tinhorns. Tinseled women, flaunting themselves and their merchandise. Barkers chanting their persuasive spiel: "Come in, gentlemen, to the Domino where the games are square and the girls are beautiful!" This was Gold Plume, wild and tough and bawdy. This was Gold Plume, Duke Madden's town.

Jim racked his horse and, ducking around a pile of lumber, stepped into a canvas-topped restaurant. Every stool along the pine counter was occupied, and Jim took his place at the end of the line of waiting miners, long experience in boom towns having built a patience that was not natural in him. Outside, a couple of riders were pushing a dozen small steers through the burros and horses, cursing and being cursed. Jim, looking out, saw with some surprise that the steers carried the Rocking C brand.

The line moved up and presently Jim had a stool. "Steak, fried potatoes, and coffee," he said. As he ate, he thought about Belle Calvert's steers. Two-year-olds, he judged. With the amount of hay he had seen below the Rocking C ranch house, it struck him that it was a fool thing to be selling the steers now. Another six months would put weight on them, but the girl had impressed him as one who knew her business.

Jim had a slab of peach pie. He ate slowly, savoring the sweetness, the long trail and hot days giving him an appetite for it. When he was done, he made way for a miner, and asked: "How much?"

"Five dollars," the aproned man said.

Scowl lines marked Jim's forehead. "Ain't that a mite high?"

"Good meal, wasn't it?"

"Hell, yes, but five dollars. . . ."

"You making trouble?"

"I'll pay, and get my next meal somewhere else." Jim slammed the money on the counter. "You're a damned thief, mister."

16

A miner elbowed Jim's ribs. "Shut up, friend."

The restaurant man scooped up the money. "Go somewhere else and be damned. I don't want your business. I've got plenty."

Jim went out into the sunlight, temper knotting his nerves. This, he guessed, would be Duke Madden's work. It surprised him because Madden had never been more than a sharp operator of gambling schemes.

"You pay high prices for everything in this camp." The miner who had elbowed Jim in the restaurant stood beside him. "If you squawk too loud, you're likely to come up in the creek with a slug in your head."

"Madden?"

"Him and Boomer Burke and their wolf pack," the miner said bitterly. "They're squeezing the camp dry. Ain't enough gold on the creek to pay the kind of prices they ask."

"Madden's a gambler. What's he got to do with the price of a meal?"

"He's organized the businessmen. Every new man who comes in has to satisfy Madden or he don't get started."

"And if they don't stick with the price agreement, they'll get a slug in the back?"

"That's right." The miner pinned gray eyes on Jim. "You knew Madden?"

Jim nodded. "In Montana. He won't last long here."

"Looks plumb permanent now. The only way to beat him is with a vigilante organization, but we haven't got a man who can run one."

Jim told himself that Duke Madden was the problem of the men who had their stakes here, that it was nothing to him one way or another. He said—"You'll find your man when you get tired enough of Madden."—and turned away.

"Hold on." The miner fell into step with Jim and held out

his hand. "I'm Ira Raeder. Got the Blue Bonnet Mine up the gulch that ought to make me rich and won't as long as Duke Madden calls the turn."

Jim shook Raeder's hand and gave him his name. He liked the man. Raeder's grip was firm and his eyes had a way of meeting Jim's squarely.

"It'll catch up with Madden," Jim said.

"Not until it's too late for the rest of us. Harrigan, you look tough enough to do this job. Say the word and I'll get a dozen miners together tonight that we can trust. We'll have to know more about you, but I think you'll do. I don't often go wrong on a man."

Jim shook his head. "I'm no miner, and this camp don't make any difference to me. When I do the job I came here to do, I'll drift."

"We'll pay you," Raeder urged.

"No, thanks."

They walked in silence for a time, Jim's eyes raking the street for Rush Kane, Raeder eyeing Jim as if cudgeling his mind for something that would win the tall man over. As they came to the log butcher shop crowding the plank walk, Jim saw the Rocking C steers held in a pole corral along the creek. The two riders who had delivered the beef were inside, one a tiny bowlegged man with frosty green eyes and a deep-lined face, the other a club-footed cowboy who was backing away from the counter and trying to pull the little rider with him.

"Another Madden job," Raeder breathed. "The little gent is Half Pint Ord, the other one Limpy Sanders. Ord came into this country with Sam Calvert ten years ago."

The butcher behind the bar was one of the biggest men Jim had ever seen, tall and heavy-boned and meaty. He was laughing now, great head thrown back, little red-flecked eyes almost lidded shut. He motioned to a pile of gold eagles.

"Take it and drift, Ord. That's the price Madden says to pay, and, by hell, that's what we will pay."

Ord shook free of Sander's grip. "You offered Belle a hundred dollars a head. Now you're trying to pay half of that."

"Madden cut the price," the butcher said blandly.

"Come on," Sanders begged, pulling at Ord again.

"You're as big a thief as Madden!" Ord bellowed.

"Thief am I?" the butcher rumbled, and moved ponderously around the pine counter like a heavy locomotive going into a hard pull. "I don't take that off nobody, including runts and cripples."

"Stand pat!" Ord called, and grabbed his gun.

The butcher moved with surprising speed for a man of his size. His right hand smashed downward across Ord's frail wrist as his left hand clubbed him on the side of the head. The little cowboy went down into a still, twisted pile.

The temper that had been in Jim Harrigan since he had clashed with Boomer Burke broke now. Forgetting that this was none of his business, he stepped into the butcher shop, gun palmed.

"That'll be enough, mister," Jim said flatly.

The butcher had started toward Limpy Sanders who was backed against the wall. Now he came to a flat-footed stop. He put his gaze on Jim, rage staining his face and slowly spreading to the back of his neck. "Why are you horning in?" he demanded.

"Makes you no never mind why I'm in. If you've killed that cowhand, I'll see you hang. If you made a deal for one hundred dollars a head, you'll keep it."

"You're wrong, friend." Crooked snags of teeth showed in a wicked grin. "Mebbe you don't know that Duke Madden sets the prices and we pay 'em. If you've got an argument, go over to the Domino."

"You owe twelve hundred." Jim nodded at Sanders. "That right?"

"That's it."

"Pay him." Jim motioned to the butcher.

"Go to hell," the giant bellowed.

"I'll give you ten seconds. Got a watch, Raeder?"

"You bet I have," Raeder said exultantly.

"Start timing," Jim said coldly. "If you haven't showed that *dinero* when the time's up, you'll have a hole in your guts."

The butcher rumbled a defiant oath, gaze leaping from Raeder to Jim and back. Then he broke, bravado seeping out of him like wheat pouring from a cut sack. He counted out another $600 and handed it to Sanders.

"Give him the other stack," Jim ordered.

Still cursing, the man obeyed. Ord was sitting up now, rubbing his head.

"Help him on his horse." Jim nodded at Sanders. When the Rocking C men had gone, he slid his gun into leather. "If you want a fair draw. . . ."

"Not me," the butcher snarled, "and you'll wish to hell you'd kept your nose clean."

"He's got a bad habit of making them kind of mistakes, Si," Boomer Burke said from the street. "I just wondered how long it would take you to kick up a fracas, Jim, and damned if you didn't fool me. You done it sooner than I figgered."

Slowly Jim made his turn. Burke stood in the doorway, a gun in his hand, malicious enjoyment showing on his wide face.

"I'm pretty fast, Boomer," Jim said.

"Not fast enough to make a play good," Burke said. "Duke wants to see you. Come on."

20

II

Duke Madden's Domino was a long hall with a carved mahogany bar running along one side, keno tables, roulette wheels, and other gambling games in a large back room. Here was Gold Plume's one bit of glamour. Chandeliers glittered overhead. Painted women filtered through the crowd. A piano against the wall separating the gambling room from the saloon was making a faintly musical racket under the fingers of a stooped, chalk-faced man.

Burke had holstered his gun. He said: "I've got a Derringer in my pocket that makes a hell of a hole in a man's back, Jim. Don't make a wrong move."

"I like my back the way it is," Jim murmured.

"Left," Burke ordered. "Up the stairs."

Duke Madden was doing all right, Jim saw, and it puzzled him. Madden had been one of the small fry in the Montana camps where Jim had known him, but there was no doubt about him being top rooster here. Even now in what should be the slack time of day the Domino was crowded.

Jim climbed the stairs to the balcony. A row of doors ran along the wall, none of them numbered. Burke said: "First one, Jim."

Turning the knob, Jim pushed the door open and moved swiftly through it, fingers brushing gun butt. He hadn't known how he'd be received. Then his hand dropped. Duke Madden was sitting behind a roll-top desk, a sly smile twisting his thin lips.

"No rough stuff, Jim." The gambler pointed toward a leather couch. "This is just a friendly visit."

"A hell of a way to invite a man in for a visit," Jim growled.

Burke heeled the door shut. "I'd better get his iron, Duke. It was a damned fool notion letting him keep it."

"He don't want to die bad enough to make a draw." He laid his gaze on Jim's face. "Boomer tells me you've resigned."

"That's right."

Twisting his swivel chair, Madden took a cigar from the box on his desk and bit off the end. He held his silence for a moment, taking his time lighting the cigar. Jim, seated on the couch, saw that Madden hadn't changed except that his run of luck had given him an opportunity to satisfy his desire for comfort. The office was expensively furnished for a camp like Gold Plume where everything had to be packed in. The desk was mahogany, the leather covering of the couch black and of good quality. There were a number of chairs in the room, a small safe set against yonder wall, and some pictures of nude, round-figured women hanging on both sides of the door. Madden's suit was of costly black broadcloth, his white shirt silk. The diamond in the ring on his right hand was large and brilliant. He was a shrewd and elegant man, this Duke Madden, with a saber-sharp nose overlooking a carefully trimmed mustache. His obsidian-black eyes indexed his tough and unforgiving character, and now they showed a worry that was nagging him.

"Boomer and me know you didn't come to Gold Plume to look at scenery," he said finally. "I doubt like hell that you're after either of us. You dragged us back across the Bitter Roots and made us stand trial in Helena for a killing we didn't do. When we beat that charge, you were done with us."

"I know." Jim crossed his legs, smiling now as if he saw humor that escaped both Madden and Burke. "I don't see that it's any of your business why I'm here."

"Everything in Gold Plume is my business." Madden

leaned forward. "I'm riding a grizzly, and you might be the huckleberry who's aiming to stick a burr under my saddle."

"I didn't have a notion about bothering you till you put this gun dog on my tail," Jim said sourly. "I don't like that."

"I don't give a damn whether you like it or not." Madden tongued his cigar to the other side of his mouth. "I'm going to find out why you're here. I've got too good a thing to lose. I was in Durango when I heard about this strike. There weren't fifty men in the camp when me and Boomer showed up. We sunk every nickel we had into this place and kept putting our profits back. This winter we'll clean up."

"My reason for coming has got nothing to do with you," Jim said.

"I wouldn't lay a bet on that." Madden took his cigar out of his mouth. "First, you sided the Calvert girl against Boomer. Then you butted into a deal between Si Taylor and the Rocking C boys. What does that sound like?"

"I ain't one to stand still while a bunch of men push a girl around," Jim said testily, "or beat up a runt Ord's size. Now what are you going to do about it?"

"Boomer says to give you a chunk of lead where it'll hurt." Madden pulled on his cigar, found that it had gone out, and re-lighted it. "I'm not sure. As far as I'm concerned, we're dealing from a new deck."

"Fair enough." Jim rose and paced to the window. He looked down at the shifting crowd in the street. "I'm kind of curious about your scheme for cleaning up, Duke. Looks like you're milking your cow dry."

"She'll be dry by the time I'm done," Madden said with arrogant confidence. "Most of the boys in camp have money. There'll be more by spring because we've had some good strikes. With the monopoly I've got, I'll be in a position to tote the *dinero* out myself when the pass is open in the spring.

That's why I can't let you go around tripping me up."

Jim shrugged. "Seems to be your cow. Guess I'll mosey. I don't figure on being here long, so I won't bother your milking none."

"A couple of boys in the next room have got their sixes lined on your belly, Jim," Madden said coldly. "You go out of that door before I tell you to, and you won't be eating no more."

Anger crowded Jim then. That was the reason for Madden's letting him keep his Colt. His gaze swept the wall, but he could not locate the guns. They were hidden behind the red-figured wallpaper, he guessed, with tiny eyeholes too small to be seen from where he stood.

"You must like my company," Jim murmured.

"I like it well enough to keep you till I know why you're here."

"You've made money in Gold Plume, Duke. Maybe I can."

"That's no reason for a bloodhound like you. I doubt like hell that you ever resigned your marshal's job."

"Ever hear of a marshal getting rich?" Jim asked.

"Never did," Madden admitted.

"I don't want this kind of money." Jim made a sweeping gesture toward the main floor. "But I get damned tired of risking my neck for the kind of *dinero* Uncle Sam pays."

"So you came here on a job that'll pay more," Madden said with satisfaction. "You just put a gun to your head when you said that. Raeder hire you?"

"I didn't say so." Jim saw he'd made a mistake. Perhaps a fatal one. "I came here on a personal chore."

"You were talking to Raeder," Madden charged.

"He was in the restaurant when I ate dinner."

"He's been trying to organize some vigilantes," Madden

24

pressed. "You're the kind of a man he needs to boss the outfit. I won't stand for that."

"You're wasting time," Burke said impatiently. "I've had something to give this yahoo ever since he fetched us back from Idaho."

"Boomer wants your hide," Madden said softly. "Know any reason why he shouldn't have it?"

Jim could smell death now, there on the other side of the wallpaper, and it was in Duke Madden's hands whether it came snarling through with a roar and tongue of flame.

"Boomer is a pretty fair trigger boy, Duke," Jim said as if he felt he was in no real danger, "but he doesn't have your brains."

"Shut up, Boomer." Madden grinned as he tossed his cigar butt into a spittoon. "What are you getting at, Jim?"

"It's always a mistake to kill a man when you don't have to. You don't have to kill me."

"Hell, I would be a fool to let you walk out of here and start working for the vigilantes."

"I didn't make this ride for that." This was it. Either Madden believed the truth, or Jim Harrigan was a dead man. "I trailed Rush Kane here from Dodge City to kill him. When that's done, I'm drifting."

"Of all the damned hogwash!" Burke bellowed.

"Shut up, Boomer. You've got a brain like a canary." Madden reached for another cigar, a thoughtful expression on his face. "What do you want Rush for?"

"He married my sister. I guess you know what happened in Dodge City. That's why I resigned my job. I couldn't do this chore as long as I was toting my badge."

"You believe that yarn?" Burke demanded.

"He's talking straight." The sly smile was on Madden's thin lips again. "I guess we're in position to do each other a

25

good turn, Jim. I'd like to have Rush out of the way, and I'd just as soon play it your way as have one of my boys beef him."

"Say, you're talking sense now," Burke said. "Let Harrigan get Kane."

"You always were a hell of a checker player, Boomer, because you never could see more than one move ahead." Madden chuckled. "All right, Jim. You can have Rush any time you want him. You'll find him at the Rocking C."

Watching the gambler, Jim couldn't tell what was going on behind those black eyes. "I don't get this," he said. "Rush used to work for you. I figured he was heading for Gold Plume to deal for you again."

"Rush Kane will never deal for me again," Madden said feelingly. "You go ahead and do your chore. Then get to hell out of camp."

Jim moved to the door and opened it. He turned then, eyes searching the gambler's bland face. He asked: "Why would Rush head for the Rocking C?"

The cat-like cruelty that was a part of Duke Madden was mirrored now in the widening of his smile. "Natural place for him to go, I guess. He's Belle Calvert's brother, and with her behind him he may be a little hard to handle."

Pushing his way across the crowded street to his horse, Jim found himself thinking about what Madden had said. It was unbelievable. Jim had seen Belle but a few minutes, but those minutes had been long enough to convince him that she was everything that was fine and decent. It was impossible for her to have a brother like Rush Kane, but it must be true, or Duke Madden, suspecting what he did, would not have let him leave the Domino alive.

Jim mounted, and turned his roan into the southbound

flow of traffic, hardly conscious of his surroundings. He would kill Rush Kane, but he could not think past that moment, could not think of what Belle Calvert would do or what she would think, and suddenly it seemed important that Belle think well of him. Duke Madden had told him more than he had intended. Reading between the lines, he guessed that Madden had pulled off too many killings. Public opinion was something to be feared even in a mining camp like Gold Plume. He was afraid of Ira Raeder, and he was afraid to make a bold move against Belle Calvert.

As far as Madden was concerned, Jim's arrival was a gift from heaven. It would result in Kane's death, and it would keep Jim from staying to side Belle if he wanted to. That was the way the gambler had figured it, and Jim cursed him for his shrewdness.

Before Jim was out of the traffic, a mounted man spurred a horse into the street ahead of him, almost running a miner down, and took the south road in a gallop. Jim gave it little attention at the moment. He rode slowly, his thoughts sour company.

Hate did not come naturally to Jim Harrigan, but it had been a corroding bitterness in him from the moment he had learned what had happened to his sister in Dodge City. Only the death of Rush Kane would purge that bitterness. Yet, when he thought about it, he saw Belle Calvert, her black eyes and black hair, the sweet set of her mouth, and he knew he would hate himself from the moment Rush Kane went down before his gun.

He had almost reached the Rocking C when he met the man he had seen leaving town just ahead of him. Still he thought little about it, for his own problem was gripping his mind and leaving room for nothing else. Ahead of him was Rush Kane, and Rush Kane had to die.

Half Pint Ord was pulling gear off his horse when Jim rode in. He called: "Howdy, mister! Say, you sure did us a favor in town. I didn't get a chance to thank you then."

Ord came across the yard in a fast, rolling pace, a grin creasing his wrinkled face. He held out his hand, and Jim, stepping down, took it.

"Glad to do it, friend."

"You're a marked man now," the little cowboy said soberly. "Nobody bucks Duke Madden, and lives to sing about it."

"I ain't much of a songbird, anyhow," Jim said.

"Come on in. I told Belle about it, and she was sure tickled. That six hundred dollars looked plumb big to her."

Jim fell into step with Ord, resenting the cowboy's friendly manner. For an instant he didn't know why, and then he did know, and he hated himself as he had known he would. He was entering Belle Calvert's house under the guise of friendship. She'd welcome him and she'd thank him, and then he'd kill her brother. No man, he thought with inward heat, could be lower than that.

Opening the door, Ord stepped aside. "Here's the man who took chips in our ruckus, Belle."

"I've met Mister Harrigan. Come in and close the door. If you make a move for your gun, I'll kill you."

Jim blinked for a moment in the gloom of the house. Then his eyes focused clearly on her, and he felt himself shriveling like a fly before a blast of flame. She was standing against the far wall, her Winchester held on the ready. He had never seen so much contempt on a human face.

"Have you gone loco, Belle?" Ord exploded.

"Loco enough to kill him," she said grimly. "Take his iron."

"Look, Belle. This is the man who pulled his cutter on Taylor. If. . . ."

28

"He had me fooled, too. I said to take his iron."

Swearing feelingly, Ord obeyed. "It'll be a long cold day before he does you a good turn again. What's the matter?"

"He came out here to kill Rush," the girl said bitterly. "If Madden hadn't sent a man to warn us, he'd have done it."

"I'll be damned." Ord faced Jim. "That right?"

"That's right," Jim admitted.

He knew now why the man had left town ahead of him. More than that, he saw the real depth of Madden's scheming. The gambler had still been suspicious of his relationship with Ira Raeder, and he'd rigged the play this way, hoping to get rid of two men he wanted removed and still keep his hands clean.

Hate was in the room, hate and scorn that Belle and Half Pint Ord had for him, as intangible as smoke and as real. Resentment rose in him then. "Maybe I look like a skunk, but I don't smell like one," he said hotly. "Rush Kane needs to die. If I'd caught him on the street, I'd have killed him the same as I would any sidewinder."

"Give him his gun," Belle said in sudden decision.

"Now you *are* loco!" Ord shouted. "Rush can't. . . ."

"Give it to him."

Reluctantly Ord obeyed and drew his own six. "Just one funny move, mister, and I'll forget what you done in town."

Belle motioned toward the stairs. "Rush is up there."

III

Jim went ahead of the girl, not understanding this. Nor did he understand why Rush, if he had been warned, hadn't met him in front of the house with his gun in leather ready to smoke it out.

"The room on your right," Belle said. "I want to see if you're any part of a man."

Jim stopped in the doorway, surprise holding him there. Rush Kane was in bed, a bandage around his head, his face as white as the pillow on which he lay. Pale lips pulled tight in a grin when he saw who it was. He said—"Long time no see, Jim."—and held out his hand.

"He's not here to shake your hand," Belle said in quiet fury. "He's here to kill you."

Kane's arm dropped, pleasure washing out of his face. "I guess you've got something wrong."

Jim stepped in the doorway, surprise making him suddenly weak and foolish. He had known Rush Kane as a tall, vigorous man, filled high with the love of life, a strong man and an honest gambler. Finding him this way was something that had never entered his mind.

"You can put down your Winchester, ma'am," Jim said heavily. "What's between me and Rush will wait till he's on his feet."

"What's this all about?" Kane asked.

Jim came to stand at the head of the bed. "You knew what I thought of Ann," he said dully. "I respected you when you married her, but I reckon I had you pegged wrong. Ann wrote that your luck had run out. When I got there, I found you'd killed her."

Kane flinched as if he'd been struck. "If that's what you

30

believe, then go ahead and do what you came to do."

"Isn't that what happened?" Jim demanded roughly.

"No. If I never had another decent thing in me, my love for Ann was decent and fine and beautiful. I'd have killed myself before I'd have knowingly let anything happen to her."

"Sure, you didn't hold the gun." Jim gestured impatiently. "But you got into a ruckus and killed a man. Then you high-tailed to your room, thinking that with Ann there they'd let you alone, but they came after you and Ann was shot. In my book that says you killed her."

Kane closed his eyes. "Go ahead, Jim, if it's what you believe."

Jim stared at the still, white face of this man he had planned to kill, and for the first time doubt rose in him. "I'll listen to your yarn, Rush," he said at last.

"Go to hell," Kane whispered. "You wouldn't believe anything I said."

"I'll tell you what happened!" Belle cried, crossing the room to face Jim. "An honest gambler didn't have a chance in Dodge City. Not with the sharpers he was playing with. He lost everything he had, and then he got my letter telling him Dad had been killed and that Duke Madden was here. I asked him to come and help. He didn't have any money to bring Ann, and he couldn't leave her there, so he tried to use the same tricks that had been used against him."

"I'm not a very good gambler, Jim," Kane whispered. "I wasn't smart enough to catch them, and I wasn't smooth enough to keep them from catching me. One man pulled his gun, and I got him. I thought that ended it, but they followed me to the room. When they yelled to come out, Ann tried to make me stay inside. They shot through the door, and she got hit."

"You rode off," Jim accused bitterly. "You didn't have the

guts to stay and bury her."

"Ann was dead, and I couldn't help her then." Kane motioned to Belle. "She needed me. I killed the two men who shot Ann, and rode out of town. I couldn't have done anything more." He opened his eyes and looked at Jim, self-condemnation on his face. "I've never been worth a damn. Dad said that when I left here. I should have been shot when I married Ann. Now go ahead and get it over with."

Rush Kane's eyes closed as if the effort of keeping them open was too much for him. There was silence; the metallic beating of the clock on the bureau was the only sound in the room. Some of the long pent-up hatred drained out of Jim Harrigan then. They might have lied to him back in Dodge City, friends of the men Kane had killed. Yet, staring down at this man who seemed close to death, Jim couldn't bring himself to say he believed him.

"I wouldn't kill you when you're lying here like this," Jim said finally and with some anger. "You know that. I've got some thinking to do."

Kane looked at him then. "I was hoping you'd take the job I fizzled at. The man who needs killing is Duke Madden."

"That's why Rush is this way," Belle cried. "When I told him all that had happened, he went to see Madden. He told him he'd get proof that Madden had killed Dad. They drygulched him on his way back."

"A fool way to go at it," Jim said.

"I've been crazy ever since I lost Ann," Kane muttered.

Belle motioned toward the door. "That's enough talk."

When they were downstairs, Jim said thoughtfully: "Madden told me where I'd find Rush. Then he sent word out here I was coming, figuring that maybe we'd both get plugged, but I can't figure out why with Rush shot up like this."

"Madden doesn't know how bad Rush is. I asked the doctor not to tell."

"What are his chances?"

Belle gestured wearily. "Doc wouldn't say." She hesitated, glancing at Ord and then back to Jim. "What are you going to do while you wait for Rush to get well so you can kill him?"

Jim paced across the room to stare out of the window. Sunlight had fled from the cañon floor, and evening shadows were thickening into dusk. The knifing sharpness of her words curried his nerves raw. Without turning, he said: "I don't know."

"Madden will kill you if you go back to town," she pressed.

"It might work the other way. Mebbe I'll kill Madden."

"That's what Dad thought. He got ten thousand dollars for the town site and some cattle. Then he was robbed. He accused Madden, and the next morning we found his body between here and Gold Plume."

Jim turned then. "I'm sorry."

"Dad should have known," she said miserably, "that one man can't touch Madden. You ought to know it, too."

"Your dad was a rancher. I've been a lawman. That makes a difference when you buck a tough like Duke Madden."

"Not enough difference."

Ord had slipped out through the kitchen. From where he stood at the window, Jim couldn't see Belle's face clearly, but he felt that she was watching him, weighing him, perhaps hoping that he was a different man than she now judged him to be.

"It's an old game with me," he said. "When you fight a man who has the grip Madden has, you don't go at it the direct way. You whittle him down first."

33

"Then you are going to fight Madden?"

He felt the tension that was in her, the expectancy. He sensed again, as he had the first time he had seen her, that here in Belle Calvert were the qualities he had dreamed of finding in a woman. He had never had time to look for them before, and he had always thought that a lawman, risking his life as he did, had no right to ask a woman to be his wife. That was behind him. His life was his own now, to live as he saw it, to take what he wanted. Here she was, and she might have loved him if a perverse fate had not dealt him the hand it had. Now she could only hate him.

"I guess I don't have much choice," he said at last. "I ain't in the habit of running when a man rigs up a play like Madden did today."

"I have your word you won't harm Rush now?"

"Yes."

"I hope you'll stay for supper, Mister Harrigan. I know how Duke Madden can be licked."

Jim sat on the front steps, smoking, while the last bit of daylight left the cañon and heat fled with the light and a chill wind swept down from the peaks above him. He tried to bring his mind to focus on Rush Kane, to form a sane judgment, but could not. His thoughts were turbulent whirlpools, always sweeping back to Duke Madden. The desire for vengeance that had been a driving force in him these last days had subsided until it was a mere spark beside a roaring flame, this need for smashing Duke Madden.

Jim had no idea how Belle meant to fight Madden, but he made his own plans, and he was still thinking about them when she called him to supper. Half Pint Ord and the crippled rider, Limpy Sanders, ate with them. Jim had liked Ord from the moment he'd seen him make his stand against the

34

butcher, and at the same time had instinctively distrusted Sanders. He was a sullen man, keeping his face lowered over his plate while he ate.

When they had finished eating, Jim asked: "What's your plan for whipping Madden?"

"With food," she said. "It's that simple. We sold our last steers today to get money to buy another herd and drive them into the valley before the pass is blocked. Winter shuts us in unless you want to go out on snowshoes and risk the slides. Most of the miners won't do that, so by spring they'll have to pay what Madden and his organization asks for food."

"And you'll control the only supply of meat that Madden doesn't."

She nodded. "We've got plenty of hay to winter two hundred head. We can buy cattle cheap in Utah, and by doing our own slaughtering we can undersell Madden's butchers, and still make a profit."

"Even at Utah prices, twelve hundred dollars won't buy many steers."

"We've made other sales," she said quickly. "Not for as good a price as you wangled out of Taylor, but enough to buy two hundred head."

It would work if Belle Calvert had enough men to hold her cattle until the day when winter privations and Madden's greed forced Gold Plume to come to her. Jim knew that because he'd been in snow-bound mining camps, and he'd seen the fantastic prices that the threat of starvation forced people to pay. But he knew, too, that long before that day Madden would act in a drastic and unpredictable manner.

Jim shot a glance at Sanders, but he still couldn't see the man's eyes because his head was bowed over pipe and tobacco pouch. He said: "It's late in the year to make a drive like that."

"I know," Belle said, "but some falls the snow comes late. We'd have to gamble on that."

Jim rose. "I've got a better notion. Want to ride to town with me, Ord?"

"Sure." The little cowboy came to his feet. "Gonna make a call on Madden?"

Sanders's head had snapped up. He sat motionlessly, his filled pipe and tobacco pouch held in front of him, interest lines deep around his brittle, glass-sharp eyes.

"I was hoping you'd go to Utah with the boys," Belle said, disappointment honing an edge to her voice.

"If you're dealt two hands, you play the best one first. Come on, Ord."

Jim waited until they were in the saddle before he asked: "How long has Sanders been with you?"

"He rode in just after Sam was killed. All the old hands but me had drawed their time to take a crack at the mines. Limpy asked for a job, and Belle was glad to have him. He's a good hand, Harrigan."

"You trust him?"

Ord hesitated as if choosing his words carefully. "Sometimes when you don't have a sharp blade handy, you have to use a dull one. Or maybe one that ain't tempered right and snaps off in your hand. Might even fly up in your face. Can't tell till you try it."

The old rider's implication was plain enough. As far as he was concerned, Limpy Sanders could be trusted—about as far as Jim Harrigan could.

"You know Ira Raeder?"

"You bet. A top hand gent, Ira is, and a good friend of Belle's. He liked her dad. Prospected all through the San Juan before he made the strike here. Stayed at the Rocking C whenever he came through."

36

"He's the man I want to see. Know where his cabin is?"

"Right up the gulch."

Gold Plume was simmering when they rode through; within the hour it would be boiling. Traffic ebbed and flowed along the plank walk; men elbowed and rammed their way from one saloon to the other, finally coming to Madden's Domino. Flares threw a leaping, lurid light across the street, and barkers intoned their persuasive chants into the laughter and curses and ribald song that rose from the crowd.

"Spend their days in the bowels of the earth," Ord said sourly, "and their nights in hell making Duke Madden rich."

The business block fell behind, and they were threading their way through the miners' shacks and tents when Ord said: "Here it is."

There was no light in it. Disappointment knifed through Jim. "He ain't there."

"That's damned funny," Ord said thoughtfully. "Ira ain't one to go sashaying around at night."

"Maybe he's out visiting someone," Jim suggested.

"Maybe. Reckon it'd be all right to go in and wait a spell."

They dismounted in front of Raeder's cabin. Jim laid a hand on Ord's arm. "Wait," he said softly.

"What's up?"

"I had a notion I saw a man's face at the window. Too dark to be sure."

"Wouldn't be Raeder. He ain't the kind who sits in the dark and looks out at folks who ride up."

"Something's wrong, Ord. You get a feeling about things like this when you pack a star for a while."

"Hell, let's go see."

"And get some round windows in our skulls."

They held their position beside the horses, listening and hearing nothing but the business block. It was dark, no moon shining between the high cliffs and only a narrow patch of black sky set with a few stars. Miners' cabins on up the creek held lighted windows, pinpoints piercing the thick night.

"Black as the inside of a bull's gut," Ord said. "You couldn't see no face."

Jim didn't argue. It might be only the work of overly tight nerves, but he'd learned years ago that careless men didn't live long at this game. He said loudly: "Guess Ira ain't here." Then he whispered: "Take the horses up the creek. Stay there till you hear me holler or hear some shooting."

Ord grumbled a curse and obeyed. Jim dropped flat and bellied toward the cabin. Before the sound of hoofs had died, he plucked his gun, and jerked the door open with his left hand.

He called—"Hello, Raeder!"—and dived for the window.

The response was instant, and not the kind of greeting that would come from Ira Raeder. Jim reached the window as the gunman inside blasted his third shot through the doorway. Jim fired from where he stood, targeting the spot where the gun flash ribboned out. He put three more bullets into the room, firing low and spreading them two feet apart. Moving back to the door, he waited there while he heard the man die.

"All right, Harrigan?" Ord asked, coming back with the horses.

Miners were pouring out of their cabins and running toward Raeder's place, filling the air with shouted questions. Still Jim waited until half a dozen men had gathered. Then he struck a match and went in. Lighting a lamp that he found on a pine table, he heard Ord cry out. He turned, and saw Ira Raeder lying on his back in the corner, a gaping knife wound in his abdomen. Another man lay against the far wall, a bullet hole in his chest. Both were dead.

"It's Grizzly Brashada," a miner said bitterly.

"Madden's man?" Jim asked.

Puzzled, they stared at him for a long moment before one asked: "How did you know, stranger?"

"I know Madden. You'll have killings like this as long as he rods the camp. Come on, Ord."

Duke Madden had said he had too good a thing to lose. He might have added that he'd go to any length to hold it. Riding back to the Rocking C, Jim thought bitterly he should have foreseen this and countered Madden's move. Madden was still convinced that Raeder had sent for Jim to run the vigilantes, and he'd decided to snuff out that danger permanently.

"Another five minutes and we'd have saved Raeder's life," Jim said with regret. "He propositioned me today to help organize some vigilantes, and I turned him down. Then I changed my mind after I talked to Belle. That's why I wanted to see him tonight."

"There ain't anybody else in this camp who could pick out the right men," Ord grunted. "I mean nobody who could get 'em to follow him like Ira could."

"I guess we'll play our other hand. I'll go to Utah with you, Ord."

IV

They ate breakfast by lamplight that morning. When they were done, Belle handed a heavy money belt to Ord. "You'll carry that, Half Pint. Top Zachary Rule's herd, and make the best deal with him you can." She brought her gaze to Jim. "You'll give the orders. Travel as fast as you can, even if you take all their fat off. We'll put it back after you get here, but you may not get here at all if you don't beat the snow."

"Damned fool thing to be taking orders from this yahoo when he came here gunning for your brother," Sanders said sullenly.

"Perhaps it is," Belle said. "There's one way to find out."

"How do you know he ever handled cattle?" Sanders pressed.

"Have you, Jim?" she asked.

It was the first time she had called him by his first name. He grinned. "A little."

"Rush has told me a good deal about Jim Harrigan, Limpy." Belle pinned her gaze on Jim's face. "You see, he worships you. Perhaps because you're Ann's brother, or perhaps because of you yourself."

He was yet to be tested. Again Jim sensed that Belle hoped he was the man she had first taken him to be. He said now: "The herd will come through."

"I still don't like it," Sanders said doggedly.

"You can draw your time."

"Let it go." Sanders turned to the door. "I was thinking about you."

Jim lingered until Sanders and Ord were gone. Then he asked: "I thought I heard a man ride in after I went to bed."

40

"It was Limpy. He went into town for a drink." She caught his arm. "Why, Jim?"

"Just curious." He stood at the door a moment, filling his mind with the picture of her. Then he left, certain that the threat of treachery would ride with them to Utah.

They were atop Star Mountain Pass before the sun showed a complete circle above the east wall, the cañon bottom still dark with shifting purple shadows. A chill wind knifed them when they reined up to blow their horses, and Jim pulled his collar around his neck. There had been no word spoken since they had stepped into saddles. Now Jim put his gaze directly upon Sanders's dark saturnine face.

"You ain't fooling me, Limpy. If you've got a notion about playing Madden's game, you'd better pull out now while you can still ride."

"You two would play hell trailing two hundred head from Utah," Sanders sneered. "I ain't playing Madden's game no how."

"I like to let a man know where he stands. The first trick you pull that looks off-color will get you a slug in the brisket."

"Save your lead, Harrigan."

"Let's ride." Jim turned his roan down the west slope, having one look across the great vastness of sage and piñon and cedars to the sky-reaching La Sal Mountains that sprawled across the Utah/Colorado line. Then the fast-dropping trail brought them into the spruce, and the distance was blotted out.

Ord took the lead because it was an old trail to him, paying no attention to Sanders's grumbling that it "sure as hell ain't no rack track." They came down into the flame-tinted aspens and scrub oak, reached the San Miguel that rushed toward a distant sea through red-flecked cañon walls, and made camp that night beside its singing waters.

41

They were in the saddle again by dawn, angling up the south wall, and rode westward across a sagebrush plain, slashed by innumerable cañons into a series of sweeping downgrades and steep uplifts. Southward, Lone Cone stood gracefully sharp against a cloudless sky.

It was a raw wild land holding a primitive challenge, and on another day Jim Harrigan would have thrilled to it, but now the need for haste was a never-ceasing prod. They reached the Río Dolores—River of Sorrows, named by the Spaniards a century before—and went on across the south slope of La Sal Mountain into the weird red-rock country of eastern Utah.

Beyond Moab they came to Songbird Creek and the Bridlebit Ranch. Here Half Pint Ord dickered with Zachary Rule. "I want good steers," he said. "The top of your herd. We aim to push hell out of 'em until we get 'em across Star Mountain into Gold Plume."

Zachary Rule, who ran a good Mormon outfit by strict Mormon standards, lifted his gaze to a cerulean sky. "Mebbe you'll get 'em across before snow flies. Mebbe." And the way he said it told Jim he didn't have the faintest hope they would.

It took a day to cut out the steers Ord selected, a precious day that could not be picked up on the trail. Here, beside the red waters of Songbird Creek hemmed in by red walls fringed with needles and spires and strange figures resembling ancient gargoyles that grinned down from lofty perches, riders twisted and wheeled their mounts, working out the cattle Ord wanted. Dust rose over the bawling, shifting mass, and hung there in the still air like a red, sun-bright blanket.

They were on the move at dawn, north, and then east, letting the cattle run their fractiousness out. Back across La Sal Mountain, Ord riding point, and on to the Río Dolores. The

cattle slowed with that first burst of energy gone. Then they
had to be pushed. No time to feed. Cover as many miles as
they could between sunup and sundown. That was the only
goal. Through scrub brush. Broken country. Through the
cedars. Black stands of piñon. Holding them at night in a box
cañon, if they could find one, logs and brush dragged across
the mouth. In saddles by dawn. Pushing. Always pushing
while days fled and the nights grew colder and the chances of
winning this gamble grew less with each passing hour. Always
Jim Harrigan slept with a sixth sense alive, for the danger of
Limpy Sanders's treachery was a live and constant thing.

But Jim had no fault to find with Sanders's work. He was
in the saddle as many hours as the others, and he had stopped
his grumbling. They reached the San Miguel and then it
rained. Jim, looking eastward to the mountain pass, saw the
shifting ominous clouds, and knew that it had snowed.

Still they pushed. Hoofs sucked in the mud. The river ran
high and murky. The sky cleared and it grew cold and Jim,
lifting his eyes again, saw the white hoods that fitted the
mountains like new mantles. Then they were at the foot of
Star Mountain. If their luck held, they'd drive into a Rocking
C pasture by another sundown.

"We're licked," Sanders growled that night as they hunkered beside the fire, the wind a bitter cutting blast as it
rushed down from the snow peaks.

Jim stared at him in surprise. "What's the matter with you,
Sanders? We ain't licked by a hell of a long way. Tomorrow
we'll shove 'em over the hump."

Sanders rose, eyes turning from Jim to Ord and back, the
firelight a shifting scarlet on his stubble-black face. "You
think we're not licked. Hell, man." He motioned toward the
herd held in a box cañon behind him. "They ain't et a
mouthful since we left Utah. Ganted up till there ain't

nothing but hide and bone, neither. Now you think you can push them critters through the snow." He shook his head. "I'm done."

Jim and Ord were on their feet, as tired and tight-nerved as Sanders. Clothes ragged. Stubble long on gaunt faces. Covered with the dust and grime of these days on the trail. Wanting nothing so much as sleep and more sleep. But neither had complained. Luck had been better than they had expected.

Jim, watching Sanders closely now, wondered about this sudden rebellion. Ord had guessed the snow would not be more than six or eight inches. Unless it was a good deal deeper, there would be no great trouble on the pass. It was strange that Sanders hadn't quit back along the trail instead of waiting until they were within a day's drive of Gold Plume, and Jim thought he could guess the reason. This would be as good a place as any for Madden to steal the herd, a great deal safer than after it had reached the Rocking C.

Sanders did not move. He had made a statement, and now stood motionlessly, sullen eyes meeting Jim's as if waiting to see what action his words would provoke.

It was Ord who broke the silence. "Them steers ain't as bad off as you're letting on, Limpy, and neither are we. Hell, we ain't been on the trail long. It just ain't sense for you to quit."

"I figgered we'd beat the snow," Sanders grunted.

"All right," Jim said in sudden decision. "Ride and keep going. Don't let me catch up with you."

"I'll wait till morning." Sanders began backing away from the fire.

"You're getting out now." Jim motioned toward Sanders's horse. "Go on, drift."

Sanders pulled at an ear, belligerence seeping out of him.

44

"Reckon I'll stay. We might get through. No use throwing a good job away."

"If you're staying," Jim warned, "don't ride out during the night."

Jim made his bed close to the cliff, wondering about Sanders and seeing little logic in his actions. The treachery he had expected had not materialized. Weariness and the nearness to trail's end had relaxed his vigilance. Now his nerves were tight as a fiddle string again. He moved his bed farther along the cliff when he heard Sanders snore, and dropped into a light sleep.

Jim was never sure what woke him. It might have been a stirring of the cattle. A strange movement in the brush. A splash in the river. He sat up, senses alert, silently drawing his gun. Overhead a round moon laid a platinum shine upon the water, and the aspens, stripped now of most of their leaves, ranged up the mountainside like countless ghosts on the march, the wind whispering through them.

Then he caught the sound of movement upstream, and called: "Who is it?"

A ribbon of flame leaped at him and a bullet snapped past. His answering fire was quick and accurate. Limpy Sanders came up on tiptoes and reeled away from the shadowed cañon wall to sprawl out fully, his head almost falling into the hot ashes of the fire.

Jim moved position quickly, keeping the cliff to his back. More guns opened up, Ord's on the other side of the fire, and at least three men in front of him. Lead chipped the rock behind Ord and screamed away into the night. Jim dropped to his knees, holding his fire, and mentally cursed Ord for giving away his position.

It was an old game to Jim Harrigan, and one that he understood well. Experience had taught him not to waste a bullet.

45

Ord's gun, too, had gone silent. Confident that their raking fire had done its work, the three left the cover of the boulders near the river and came toward the cliff. In that instant Jim's gun became a leaping, living thing, foot-long tongues of flame lashing from its muzzle, its thunder rolling waves of sound beating against his ears.

One man jackknifed at the knees and went down. Another threw a wild, hurried shot at Jim and took a slug in the chest. The third made a run for it along the edge of the river. Jim fired at him and missed. It was Ord who drove two bullets into him, caused him to break stride, stumble, and topple into the swift-running river.

"You all right, Ord?" Jim called.

"Got a nick in my left arm's all. I figgered they got you after you downed Limpy."

Jim walked to where Sanders lay and rolled him over. "Dead," he said, and pulled him away from the fire. He glanced at his watch. "Be sunup in an hour or so. We'd better get breakfast and start 'em moving."

"I reckon." Ord stared at Sanders's face, sullen in death as it had been in life. "What in hell was biting that coyote?"

"He went to town the night Raeder was killed. I'm guessing he saw Madden and told him what Belle was figgering on. Chances are they rigged this then, aiming to salivate us and take the herd."

"What was his idea for trying to quit?"

Jim shrugged. "Hard to tell. Maybe he aimed to worry us. Or maybe he wanted to ride off and meet these *hombres* up on the pass. Then he got boogery and changed his mind. Not much bottom. Never is in men who hire out to double-cross somebody."

Dawn was breaking across a bright cold sky when they cleared the mouth of the box cañon and started the herd. It was steady pushing, the snow at first a thin sprinkle like stingy frosting on a cake. Gradually deepening, it slowed but didn't stop them. They topped the pass shortly after noon, and came out of the snow. It was dusk when they reached the valley floor and shoved the herd into a pasture behind the Rocking C buildings.

Belle had steaks sizzling when they came into the house. She stood at the stove, staring at their bearded faces as if she found it hard to recognize them, a tight worry in her face Jim had not seen before, her shoulders drooping a little as if some pride had gone from her.

"You've got your steers," Jim told her, "and I don't reckon it'll take many days to put some taller on 'em."

"Where's Limpy?"

Jim told her while she forked the steaks onto a platter. Then he asked: "How's Rush?"

She faced him now, lips trembling as she fought to control her emotions. When she did speak, it was a whisper that barely reached him. "I don't know. He went to town yesterday, and hasn't come back."

V

Jim ate hungrily and went to bed. Bone-weary, he gave little thought to what Belle had said. He slept like a dead man, and woke to look upon a white world. They had beaten the snow by hours.

Ord was finishing breakfast when Jim came into the kitchen. "Some lazy devils can sleep all day," he said amiably, "but I've got cattle to feed."

Jim grinned and rubbed a hand across his whiskery face. "Sure, I slept all day. Must be almost daylight now." He pulled a chair up to the table. "You'd have to put snowshoes on them critters to get 'em over the hump now."

"Lucky all the way." Ord rose and moved to the door. "If you ain't above it, Harrigan, you can come out and give me a hand."

"I ain't above it, but I got another job that needs doing first. Bringing the beef in ain't much good if we don't fix Madden. I wish Raeder was alive."

"There's talk that you killed him," Belle said.

Her words jolted breath from him. He stared at her blankly.

Ord, still standing at the door, cursed softly. "There's no sense in that, Belle. Jim didn't even go inside the cabin till there was five or six of us there with him."

"I'm just telling you what I heard." Belle set a plate of food in front of Jim. "There was some pretty wild talk the day you left, most of it against Madden. Then the story got started that he'd sent Brashada to ask Raeder to see him, and, while Brashada was there, Jim came in, shot Brashada and knifed Raeder. One of the miners said he saw you step out of the

48

cabin and wait until the rest came."

"That sure is a bucket of hogwash!" Ord exploded.

"It's the talk," Belle said soberly. "You can't go into town, Jim. Madden's men will lynch you."

Ord grinned crookedly. Before he went out, he said: "You'll find another pitchfork in the barn, Jim."

Jim ate slowly, thinking about this and knowing that no matter how illogical it was, Madden, with enough free whiskey and enough talk in the right places, could make this accusation stick. If Jim was found dangling from a rope some cold morning, no one would connect Madden with it.

Belle filled Jim's coffee cup, and poured another for herself. "What are you going to do about Rush?" she asked, coming back to the table.

"I ain't had much time to think about it," Jim answered evasively.

She stirred her coffee, misery-filled eyes on him. "Rush wasn't as badly hurt as the doctor thought. He'd been up a couple of days when we heard this talk about your killing Raeder. Rush couldn't stand it. He said this wasn't your fight in the first place, and he wasn't going to sit around and wait for you to come back to a rope."

"That's why he went to town?" Jim asked, thinking that Rush might have had another reason for leaving.

She nodded. "I don't suppose he's alive now."

It was a funny hand fate had dealt Jim Harrigan. He lowered his eyes thinking of the one compelling urge that had driven him to Colorado after he had looked at his sister's grave in Dodge City and heard the story of her death. Yet now the urge was gone. Hate had been a lever burning high in him, and then breaking.

He knew what Ann would tell him if she were here: that he wasn't God, that revenge was not for human hands. Besides, she loved Rush Kane, and what woman would do less for the man she loved than she had tried to do for Rush?

"I'll find out why he ain't back," he said at last.

"And if he's alive, you'll kill him," she said tonelessly.

Jim built a cigarette, his chair canted back against the wall, his mind reaching into his memory to the day when Ann had come to him in Helena and told him she was leaving with Rush. Jim had told her she was crazy to follow him, that she should stay in Helena where she had her home.

"You've never been in love," Ann had said simply. "When you are, you'll know what it means to be with the one you love, to work for that person, and maybe die for him."

She had done exactly that, and he knew she would have no regrets. Whatever blame could be laid upon Rush Kane, killing him would not bring Ann back. He saw himself in a new light, saw the corrosive effect of the hate that had been sucking at him through these weeks.

"I guess me and Rush won't have any trouble," he said.

"Jim." Belle leaned forward, elbows on the table. "You came here to kill Rush and instead you risked your life going after my cattle. Why?"

He couldn't tell her. She wouldn't believe it. Or if she did, her answer to his question would be no. She couldn't love a man who had come so close to killing her brother. So he said lightly: "Madden shoved me around. Now I'm going to do the shoving. See if you can find some paper and a pen and ink."

When she brought them, he pushed the paper to her. "Put this down, will you? Nobody can read what I write."

For half an hour he paced the floor, smoking steadily, having her write and scratch out and rewrite until she had what he wanted. Then he read it through again.

How long will you accept one man's rule?

How long will you pay high prices for everything you buy in Gold Plume?

How long will you allow gamblers to set the prices you pay?

Rocking C has beef to sell at a fair price, but it will not have it long unless Duke Madden is licked.

Rocking C asks the help of every honest man in Gold Plume in this fight.

"It'll do," Jim murmured.

"You aren't going into town, Jim?"

"Sure." He slid into his coat. "If you listen, you'll hear Madden cuss when he reads this."

She caught his arm. "You can still get over the pass if you start now."

"I never leave a job half done." He took hold of her and pulled her against him. He saw how near she was to breaking, and yet he knew she would not break. There was a strength in her that Rush lacked. If she had been Rush, she would have stayed and died in Dodge City. It was that proud courage that had held her here after her father had been killed, had made her fight against odds that no gambler would take.

"But it isn't your job!" she cried.

"It is now." Then he forced himself to ask a question that had been in his mind all the way to Utah and back. "Would it make any difference to you if I got killed?"

She tore free and walked away. She stood for a moment facing the stove, her back to him. There was no sound but her breathing and ticking of the clock on the shelf above the table. Then, without turning, she said: "I am in debt too much to you now."

He went out and strode through the shifting white curtain

of snow to the barn. He should not have asked the question. He could not expect her to love him. He saddled and, mounting, took the road to Gold Plume, a bitterness in him that he had never felt before. Now he had a chance to live his own life, and he had found the woman who would give meaning to that life, but his hatred had killed whatever chance there had been of earning her love. And hope died then in Jim Harrigan.

Jim settled down into his coat collar, hearing the high scream of the wind, watching snowflakes whip around him in dizzy horizontal flight. Winter had come a month ahead of time. A spell of good weather might take the snow off in the cañon bottom, but it would stay in the pass. He wondered in grim relief what it was like up there now in that treeless open space that looked out upon the world.

He rode slowly when he reached town, remembering he had seen a log cabin that served as a newspaper office. Even by hugging the path that twisted along the creek side of the street, he found it hard to see the buildings, for snow was a white curtain drawn across his vision. Then, finding the cabin, he left his horse on the sheltered side, and waded through the snow to the door. He opened it, stamped snow from his boots, and slid in.

The interior of the cabin was warm and strong with the smell of ink and paper. A man sat huddled on a stool at the composing bench, straining forward to catch all of the thin light that he could. He turned when he heard the door and said—"Good morning."—in a nasal twang that marked him as an Easterner. "I mean it's a hell of a morning, isn't it?"

"It is for a fact." Jim laid his paper on the bench. "I'd like a hundred of those run off. I'll wait."

The editor read it and lifted pale blue eyes to Jim. "I can't do it. I'd be dead before night."

He was an old man from whom age and defeat had sucked away the desire for battle, but he still nursed a small pride that made him hate himself for his cowardice. His trousers were baggy and patched; his shirt collar showed careful stitching where he had whipped down the frayed threads. He had not shaved for several days, and his white stubble made a faint fringe along his cheeks and chin. The smell of cheap whiskey and chewed tobacco made a stench about him, and Jim thought sourly that he would be a poor ally at best.

"Likely I'll be in the same fix," Jim said, "but I'm risking my neck to fight the rotten deal you've got in Gold Plume. What kind of a newspaperman are you who won't do the same?"

The editor slid off the stool, lips pulling into a determined line. "The Gold Plume *Eagle* stands for justice and fair play, my friend."

"How much have you got in Gold Plume?"

The skinny shoulders sagged, and the editor turned to the window. "The snow covers a lot of filth," he murmured, "but it doesn't change it. The filth's still there. I'm too old to be a hero."

"You'll be a hero or a dead coward." Jim drew his gun and thumbed back the hammer. "Start in."

The editor wheeled when he heard the gun coming to cock. He stared at Jim's grim stubble-dark face, and fear laid hold of him. "All right," he whispered and, climbing back on the stool, began to work. Presently he reached for a sheet of paper and rolled it across the type. "Have a look at your suicide invitation," he said and, lifting the sheet, handed it to Jim.

Jim scanned it. "Run 'em off," he said laconically and, pulling a stool up to the stove, sat down. *Suicide invitation?* Well, maybe the editor was right, and it didn't make a hell of a lot of difference. His thoughts turned to Rush Kane, and he wondered where the gambler had gone. He'd run from Dodge City, and he'd likely run again.

"There you are," the editor said at length, stacking the papers on a table.

"How much?"

"Nothing." The old man chewed his lower lip. "Except the privilege of helping you. There was a time when I'd hold to a belief through hell and high water. Then I made the mistake of running, and I've been running ever since. It's kind of good to think of myself as a man again."

"No need of you getting into trouble," Jim said roughly.

"The name's Fred Webb." The old man held out a claw-like hand. "You're Jim Harrigan, aren't you?"

"How did you know?" Jim asked in surprise.

"Heard a lot about you since Ira Raeder was killed." He sliced bacon and put it on the stove. "I thought you'd be the only one with enough courage to do what you're doing."

There was more strength in this man than Jim had thought. He said: "I didn't kill Raeder."

"Didn't suppose so." Webb filled his coffee pot from a bucket and put it on the stove. "I knew Grizzly Brashada. I felt his fists the second week I was in Gold Plume after I'd printed something Madden didn't like." He grinned wryly. "What are your plans, son?"

"I aim to pass these out. After the miners read 'em, I've got a hunch Madden will get spooked and make a mistake."

Webb stood at the stove thoughtfully scratching a cheek. "The lid's off the minute you show your face on the street. If you're bound to die, lick Madden first."

"What are you getting at?"

"Don't pass those papers out yourself, or you'll die before

54

you start. I'll get the kid who sells my *Eagle*. Madden won't catch on."

Jim nodded. "All right. Get him."

"Watch the coffee and bacon." Webb pulled into his coat and went out.

Discontent grew in Jim Harrigan while he waited. It was time for action, and waiting was against his nature, but he knew the old man was right. He paced the length of the office, smoking constantly. When he'd carried a badge, he had all the agencies of the law on his side. Now he was alone except for a girl, an old cowhand, and a broken-down editor who had been aroused enough to grasp again for a departed self-respect.

And Rush Kane. Or was he an ally? Jim couldn't guess. A year ago he'd have said yes. Now Kane was unpredictable. Jim had known more than one man of promise to lack color when the final assay was made. It was even possible that Kane had gone over to Madden to escape Jim's gun.

Webb came in with a wizened, leggy boy who read the top paper, and threw Jim a broken-toothed grin. "I took a beating from Boomer Burke. It's time somebody had the guts to fight 'em."

"Pass a few of those out in the small saloons," Jim said, "and then try the Domino. Get back in an hour, and there'll be five dollars for you."

"I don't want five dollars." The boy scooped up a stack of the papers, and moved to the door. "All I want is to see you pitch some lead at Madden and Burke."

"You may get another beating if Burke gets his hands on you."

The boy grinned again. "That'll be all right if you crack a few caps."

"Let's eat," the editor said when the boy had gone.

55

Jim glanced at his watch. "I'll give him an hour," he said worriedly.

New hope burned high in him now. The old editor and the boy had taken the beatings and done nothing, but the moment somebody came along who wasn't afraid to fight, they had accepted their responsibility. There must be hundreds like them scattered in the Domino and the other saloons, in the mines, in the cabins and tents.

It was an hour that held 1,000 minutes for Jim Harrigan. He ate and paced the floor, came back to the table for another cup of coffee, and paced the floor. He worried his watch in and out of his pocket, and, when the hour was up, he reached for his coat.

"The kid should've been back. I'm gonna kick the lid off."

"Wait a minute." Webb gnawed off a chew of plug, tongued it into his cheek, and picked up a double-barreled shotgun from a back corner. "I'll go along. I never killed a man, Harrigan, but I can."

"When I came in this morning. . . ."

"I wasn't any part of a man. I was something they should have buried the day Grizzly Brashada beat me up. Kind of funny, isn't it?" He spit into a can. "You gave me back what Brashada stole."

Jim Harrigan's grin was a quick break across his dark face. The last doubt was gone. He had to win. There were hundreds in Gold Plume like Fred Webb, like the wizened, broken-toothed kid who hadn't come back.

VI

It had stopped snowing, but the wind screaming down from the high cliffs had a slashing cut to it. It broomed the snow from the street and threw it in ragged white columns against the fronts of tents and buildings, or carried it through the open spaces and piled it high against yonder cliff, leaving the street a gaping, frozen streak threading the camp. Jim held his hands in his pockets, keeping them warm against the moment when a fast draw meant victory against Duke Madden, or death for Jim Harrigan.

"Keep 'em off my back," Jim said when they reached the Domino. "I'll do the rest."

They pushed open the saloon door, a rush of wind sweeping in with them. Jim shut it, his right hand close to gun butt as his eyes scanned the packed crowd. Boomer Burke was bellied against the bar halfway along it. Duke Madden was in his shirt sleeves, his back to the door as he watched the keno game in the gambling room.

Silence spread across the saloon like a high wave spills water over a flat beach. Boomer Burke whispered— "Harrigan."—as if the word were a curse, and the whisper ran into the silence.

Slowly Duke Madden made his turn, saw who it was, and tongued his long cigar to the other side of his mouth, his inscrutable eyes giving no hint of the feelings that were in him.

Even the chalk-faced man stopped playing the piano and turned on his bench to watch Jim. There was no sound but the girl's voice at the roulette wheel: "Seventeen and black." It, too, died as Jim climbed to the bar top.

He had seen some of the papers on the floor that the boy

had delivered, he knew the seed had been planted, and he understood the silence that his entrance had brought to the big room.

"Where's the kid I sent here, Madden?" Jim demanded.

Madden shoved long white fingers into his waistband as he said carelessly: "How the hell would I know?"

Hard on Madden's words a floor man in the corner by the piano went for his gun. It was a mistake, a fatal one, and he died without firing a shot. Head thrown back, he took a wobbly step, and then his control gave way and he fell like a tent with its ropes slashed in a single stroke.

Jim swung his smoking gun to Madden. "Get the kid," he said, "or I'll drill you between the eyes."

"He's around somewhere." Madden motioned to a floor man. "See if you can find him, Pete."

Madden was playing this in his usual shrewd way so that no blame would come to him. Nor could he be held for what his employees did. The floor man who'd made his try. The barkeep who sidled back along the mahogany and was carefully lifting his shotgun when Webb pulled one trigger. The blast nearly took the barkeep's head off.

"I've got another barrel," the editor croaked. "Anybody want it?"

No one did. Silence came again as the echoes of the shotgun's roar died. Then Madden nodded at the boy who was being pushed through a door in the back.

"Here's your kid, Harrigan," Madden said coolly. "Now get out and let the boys get on with their drinking."

"I've got something to say first," Jim said. "Mebbe some of 'em didn't see the papers the kid passed out."

Light from the overhead lamps made a bright shine on the uplifted faces: gamblers' white ones, the paint and rouge on the percentage girls, miners' beards, the bronzed faces of

58

packers. Here was a cross section of Gold Plume, tough and licentious, but holding a spark of decency and a flame of resentment against Duke Madden.

"If you can handle yourself on snowshoes," Jim said, "you don't have to worry. There's plenty of grub on the other side of Star Mountain. If you're staying here all winter, you'd better start worrying because you'll be busted by spring. Either in here or paying Madden's prices. With five thousand people stuck in Gold Plume for a winter that's starting early, you don't have to be smart to see how it'll be by spring."

"That sheet the kid passed out said Rocking C had some beef." It was the big butcher, Taylor, who had tried to crook Half Pint Ord that first day Jim was in camp. "That's a lie because I bought the last Rocking C steer."

"We brought a herd in from Utah. Come out and see 'em. If they're stolen, you'll know who done it and why. In the end it'll be our beef that decides whether Madden busts you with his prices."

"You're piling it on," Madden said in his mild tone. "You reckon the boys will believe the coyote who killed Ira Raeder?"

"The coyote who killed Ira Raeder was your man, Grizzly Brashada," Jim shouted angrily, "and I killed him! Who's the *hombre* who claims he saw me come out of the cabin?"

"He ain't here!" Burke shouted.

"The hell he ain't!" a man in the gambling room cried. "Here he is, Harrigan. Mink Drusy."

Drusy was a little man who was being shoved into the saloon from the gambling room against his will. Raising bloodshot eyes, he cried: "Don't shoot me, Harrigan!"

"But you'd have hung me with your lying story!" Jim raged. "Tell the boys how you could see me in the dark that night!"

"I couldn't!" Drusy shrieked. "I lied!"

"Why?"

Drusy tried to duck behind Madden. Somebody hit him and drove him back into the saloon. He shot a glance at Burke and licked dry lips. "Burke made me."

Jim grinned. He'd planted more seed and he'd have a good crop. It was here in the faces of these men.

"Get back to your drinking, boys!" Jim called. "Don't send anybody after me, Madden, or I'll shoot their ears off."

Jim motioned for Webb and the boy to leave. Then he jumped down from the bar and backed through the door, cocked gun held hip high. Slamming the door shut, he slapped a bullet through it that sang over the heads of those inside.

"Go with Webb," Jim ordered the boy. "Webb, stay inside and keep your door locked. This'll boil up fast now."

Jim raced along the street to his horse and, swinging up, quit town at a fast pace, hoofs ringing on the frozen ground. There was no pursuit. Madden's move would come later. Under cover of darkness.

Stabling his horse, Jim went into the house to find Ord and Belle waiting beside the stove for the coffee to boil.

"What kind of a dido have you been up to now?" Ord asked.

Jim told them, and added: "The minute we shoved that herd over the pass, we put a bee inside Madden's pants and took a reef on his belt. We'll hear from him tonight."

"But you don't know what he'll do," Belle said.

"Burn our stacks," Ord suggested.

"He ain't the one to destroy anything he thinks he can get later on." Jim took the cup Belle handed him. "He'll try to get me and Ord, thinking he can make a deal then."

"I won't deal with him on any terms," Belle said.

"Then you'll get the same dose. Any place in town you can go?"

"I'm staying here."

The way Belle said it told Jim there was nothing he could say that would change her mind. He finished the coffee and set the cup on the table, feeling admiration for this girl.

"I didn't see anything of Rush," Jim said. "We'll find out tonight."

He expected her to flare up, to say he had been the one who had driven Rush from this house. But meeting his hungry searching gaze, she said simply: "We can't help Rush if Madden kills us."

"He won't," Jim said sharply. "We'll be ready for him. Fetch all the guns and ammunition you've got. Pile it on the table. Ord and me will nail up the windows. We can hold off an army for a month."

"Dad made shutters for the windows," Belle told him. "They're upstairs."

Ord had moved to the window. Now he said: "Looks like Madden's coming, Jim."

Swearing, Jim wheeled to the window. A line of horsemen, dark against the snow, were coming from town. A dozen, Jim saw, and he cursed himself for letting Madden outguess him.

"It isn't Madden's bunch," Belle said with certainty. "Those are the men Raeder would have picked for his vigilantes."

Breath came out of Jim in a long relieved sigh. "Then it's what I've been playing for. Come on, Ord."

Jim and Ord were waiting in front of the house when the riders pulled up. "We're here to do what Ira Raeder would have done if he was still alive," the leader said. "We're ashamed that a stranger had to start the job we should have done."

"I'm glad to see you," Jim said soberly. "I was beginning to think we'd bitten off too big a bite."

The spokesman looked past the corrals to where the cattle stood huddled against the cliff. "Those steers are the only food in Gold Plume Madden don't control. Our job is to protect them and you folks. How do you want us to do it?"

"Two men to stand guard," Jim said quickly. "Madden might try to burn the stacks or steal the herd. The rest of you split the breeze getting here if you hear any shooting."

"Jones. Cartwright." The leader nodded at two of his men. "Take it till midnight. We'll send two more out then." He brought his gaze to Jim. "We've got to draw or drag now after what you done today. The camp's buzzing. The boys are talking like you was Paul Revere himself. Now reckon we'd better get back. We've got fifty men to organize."

Jim watched them go, feeling the tug of doubt. A dozen men like these would be stronger than fifty uncertain ones.

"You boys stay in the barn," Jim told the two who had been left. "I'll bring your supper out. If Madden tackles the house, you light out for help."

They were hectic hours until dark, checking guns and ammunition, seeing that there was ample food and water in the house, and putting shutters into place that Sam Calvert had prepared years ago against a possible Ute attack.

It was dark when Belle called supper. Jim took food to the men in the barn and, coming back, ate with Belle and Ord.

"Madden's licked," Jim said jubilantly. "What we needed was somebody to think there was a chance of licking Madden and start organizing."

Jim's feeling was contagious. "Sure," Ord said, "we'll give 'em hell."

And for the first time since he had come back from Utah, Jim saw real hope in Belle's eyes. "I've been sorry I ever brought you into this, Jim," she said, "because I couldn't see anything but death for us. It was just that I was too stubborn to quit. Dad had so many dreams. . . ."

"*Belle!*"

It was a high cry, shrill and demanding, from somewhere back of the house. The wind had increased; there was the scream of it around the eaves that was as horrible as a banshee's wail, but this was different. It was human, yet it seemed to be something else, coming as it did with the screech of the wind.

"*Belle!*"

It came again. Closer now. Just outside the door. They sat at the table paralyzed, heads turned to catch the sound.

Then Belle whispered: "It's Rush."

Jim knew what was in her mind. If Rush was dead, this was not a human cry. But Rush wasn't dead if he could make a sound like that. With that thought, Jim knew what it was, but he was too late. Belle was out of her chair and raising the bar that held the back door.

"Wait, Belle!" Jim shouted, but there was no stopping her.

She flung the door open. Jim palmed his gun, but he was too late. They piled in, Duke Madden in front, Belle gripped tightly before him, the muzzle of his .45 shoved hard against her ribs.

"Drop your iron, Harrigan," Madden said without feeling. "Boomer was right. We should have got you when you first hit town."

Jim let his gun go. Ord, caught flat-footed, made no try for his Colt. Burke was there. The big butcher, Si Taylor. Others Jim had never seen. And back of them, a bloody bandage around his face, stood Rush Kane.

Fury rolled through Jim. "You sniveling yellow pup!" he raged. "You knew Belle would open the door when you yelled like that."

"Pretty smart, wasn't it?" Madden glowed. "Maybe a little smarter than you were when you pulled off that job you did this afternoon." He jerked a thumb at Burke. "Look around, Boomer. Some of that vigilante bunch might be inside." He grinned at Jim. "We got the two boys in the barn."

A moment before Jim had been completely confident. Now there was no hope at all. He stood there, stooped a little, his mind on the gun at his feet.

"Even the yellow bellies in this camp won't stand for you shooting a woman," Ord said hotly.

Madden's smile was quick and wicked. "No shooting, runt, but any house can have a fire, especially on a cold night."

Jim saw that it would work as perfectly as Madden had thought. They'd be slugged, and left in a burning house with no proof that Madden had been there. There would only be the ashes, and the bones of those who had died.

Burke and the others came back into the kitchen. "Empty," he said.

"Got the coal oil, Si?" Madden asked.

"Right here," the butcher said.

"Lay your gun barrel across their heads, Boomer," Madden ordered, his voice held to a casual tone. "Put Harrigan's iron in his holster. It'll look better to find their guns beside their bodies. Better put them in bed, too. Somebody might wonder why they were burned to death in the kitchen."

Rush Kane was a forgotten man, a man who had lost his right to merit others' respect. Only his eyes seemed alive in that mass of bandages, eyes of a madman who can be pilloried no more. Taylor passed in front of him, and in one quick motion Rush swept the butcher's gun from holster and, wheeling, fired at close range over Belle's head. The bullet caught Madden above the left eye.

The kitchen was an inferno then, and Rush Kane's body broke under half a dozen bullets. Jim dropped to his knees and, gripping his gun, tilted it upward and drove a slug into Boomer Burke's wide chest. Ord's thundering .45 brought Taylor down in a sweeping fall.

Lead beat at Jim. There was the numbing pain of it along his ribs and his left thigh, the warmth of spreading blood. He propped himself on one arm, still firing until his hammer dropped on an empty. The door crashed open.

Jim heard, as if from a great distance, the pound of running feet. He came flat, trying to crawl toward a gun that lay in front of him, but he never reached it. For in that moment all sight and sound died for Jim Harrigan.

Jim was in bed when he came to. He felt the house rock as a blast of wind struck, heard the low moan. Then he was aware of the lighted lamp on the bureau, of Belle sitting beside him.

"Rush?"

"Dead," she told him. "He must have gone to town after Madden, and they got the drop on him. I suppose they held him prisoner until they needed him. His face was slashed to pieces with a knife. That must have been how they got him to call out like he did."

Maybe it was good guessing. Maybe bad. He wasn't sure what Belle really thought, for she said: "Rush was always a weak one, and he never got along with Dad. That was why he left and took another name. But Dad would have been proud of him tonight."

"He died a brave man," Jim said.

"He'd have liked to hear you say that. It's given to some to be strong just like it's given some to be weak. He thought so much of you because you were strong, and I think it was why he loved Ann."

"Ord?"

"He's gone for a doctor."

He closed his eyes then. The shadow of Rush Kane was no longer between them. There were many hills along his back trail. Lonely hills. He had ridden with a badge on his shirt and a gun on his hip. He had been cursed and hated and feared. Never, in all those years, had he done anything for the love of a woman.

He opened his eyes and looked at Belle, and she must have seen what was there, for she bent and kissed him. He knew, then, that the last hill was behind him.

Twin Rocks

1

Morgan Dill rode into Twin Rocks with the full moon a bright arc along the eastern horizon. The evening light was very thin, the flaming sky above the western hills the only reminder of the nearly spent day. Morgan was tired and dirty, his buckskin gelding was dusty and sweat-gummed from the long hours on the road. They had left Steamboat Springs at sunup. It seemed a long time ago.

The banker, Dick Lamar, had sent for Morgan and told him to stay on the side streets, but Morgan with arrogant perversity ignored Lamar's advice and rode down the middle of Main Street. He glanced at the Runyan house as he passed it, thinking briefly of Molly. At one time he had been very much in love with her and had expected to marry her. She had worn his ring for two years, and then had given it back without an adequate explanation.

For a moment the old bitterness rushed back into him, then it was gone. He had left town three years ago right after they had broken up because he couldn't stand living in the same town Molly did, seeing her and knowing he had lost her, but somewhere along the line he had been able to detach himself from his memories. Now he could think of her without pain.

Molly had lived in that house all of her life with her mother and her sister Jean. Her father had died soon after Jean was born and Mrs. Runyan had raised the girls and had succeeded in thoroughly spoiling Molly. Now, looking back, he decided that he had been lucky he hadn't married her. Still, he wondered what had happened to her. Maybe she had married someone else and had several children by now.

69

He stopped at a water trough near the corner and dismounted. He drank from the pipe, sloshed water over his stubble-covered face, and let his horse drink. He stood at the end of the trough, looking along the street that had not changed in the three years he had been gone.

Suddenly he noticed that Johnny Bedlow, the barber, had just left his shop, stopped to lock his front door, and now was hurrying along the street toward Morgan. For just a moment Morgan thought about turning his back as Johnny passed. Chances were that in the thin light the barber wouldn't recognize him, then he thought, to hell with it.

Lamar's reason for his staying off Main Street wasn't good enough. All he had said was that Morgan's sister Celia was ready to make a deal for his half of the Rafter D, the Dill ranch that had been inherited by them when their father had died four years ago, and that, if Buck Armand, Morgan's brother-in-law, saw him, there would be trouble.

Johnny Bedlow had been one of Morgan's best friends and the last man in town he would turn his back on. He stepped from the street to the boardwalk, saying: "Howdy, Johnny. Long time no see." He held out his hand, but Johnny didn't take it. He simply stopped and stared as if he were seeing a ghost, then he wheeled and ran back up the street without saying a word.

"Well I'll be damned!" Morgan said aloud, staring at Johnny's back until he disappeared around the corner at the far end of the block.

He mounted and, wheeling his horse, rode along the side of the Mercantile that was on the corner. He turned into the alley behind it, thinking there was no use to worry about Johnny Bedlow, but he couldn't get what had happened out of his mind. Of all the friends he'd had in Twin Rocks, he had been sure Johnny was one he could bank on, the one who

70

would be glad to see him and give him the warmest welcome.

Morgan had never had a real enemy in his life unless it was Buck Armand. Maybe Dick Lamar, too, who used to fawn over Molly for the two years she had been engaged to Morgan. On the other hand, he'd had a number of good friends such as Johnny Bedlow and the deputy sheriff, Tully Bean.

There were many who were in between, folks who said the Dill boy never would grow up. Not bad, they said, but a hell-raiser. He'd ride into town with the Rafter D crew, shooting at the sky and yelling his head off and sending chickens squawking as they scurried off the street and making dogs dodge horses' hoofs as they ran to safety with their tails between their legs.

Part of this was just letting off steam. The rest of it was plain Dill arrogance that Morgan had inherited from his father, old Abe Dill, commonly known as Lucifer Dill. The crew, including Buck Armand, the foreman, shared Abe's arrogance. So did Morgan's sister Celia.

Morgan reined and dismounted a few feet from the back door of the bank. He grinned as he thought about Celia. Nature had sure made one hell of a mistake in deciding her sex. She should have been born a boy. She had been cut from the same pattern old Abe had and had been his favorite child. Morgan had fought with her from the day he learned to walk, but she had held her own until he was almost grown. He wondered if she lost her temper with her husband the way she used to with him.

He turned to the back door of the bank and was reaching for the knob when he heard a woman call: "Morgan! Morgan Dill!"

He wheeled away from the door, not recognizing the woman in the thin light until she had almost reached him, and then he thought it was Molly. He opened his mouth to call her by name, wanting to appear casual about meeting her, but his mouth was dry and he couldn't say anything.

Then he was glad he hadn't said anything. He realized it wasn't Molly at all, but her sister. She had changed so much he found it hard to believe it was Jean. He remembered her as a skinny schoolgirl with pigtails down her back and a wide-eyed admiration for him every time he called on Molly. Now she was a woman and a pretty one at that.

He was even more surprised at the way she greeted him. She threw her arms around him and hugged him, and then she kissed him. It wasn't an ordinary, run-of-the-mill kiss, either, but the passionate kiss of a woman who loved a man and hadn't seen him for a long time. He was too surprised to comment.

She finally drew back, whispering: "Oh, Morgan, I was afraid I was too late. I'm such a coward. I knew I had to come, but I kept putting it off, and then hated myself because I waited so long."

"So long for what?" he demanded. "And how did you know I would be here?"

"I was afraid I'd be too late to keep you from going into the bank," she whispered. "Get on your horse and ride out of town. Don't see Dick Lamar. Don't ride out to the Rafter D, either."

He shook his head. "I don't know what you're talking about, but I ain't leaving town until I've seen Lamar. He wrote to me saying that Celia wanted to settle up for my half of the Rafter D. I don't want any part of the spread because I couldn't get along with Buck Armand, so I'll take what cash I can get and mosey on."

She gripped his arms. "You listen to me, Morgan. You've been gone for three years. As far as I know, you haven't heard from anyone in the county. Even Dick wouldn't have known where you were if you hadn't got into that fight in Steamboat Springs and got thrown into jail. He wouldn't have known where to write if he hadn't seen it in the newspaper."

"You're right on one thing," he said. "I ain't heard from nobody in this burg since I left, except Lamar. But I don't see. . . ."

"Everything's changed since you left," she said. "If you stay here, you'll be killed. Or you'll kill someone and they'll hang you. I can't tell you about it now because I don't want Dick to know I'm here. If you'll come to the house, I'll tell you . . . and then you'll have to leave town."

"I won't leave town until I've seen Lamar," he said stubbornly.

"Did he tell you what kind of a deal Celia will give you?" she asked.

"No, but my half of the Rafter D ought to be worth twenty-five thousand dollars," he said. "Maybe more, but I'll take less just to get some cash, and then I'll stay away from here the rest of my life."

"You're a fool," she said, exasperated. "You never could savvy a man like Dick Lamar. He's a liar and a cheat and a thief. I can't prove those things, but I *know* he's all of them. Stay away from him, Morgan. You don't know how to handle a slimy crook like that."

"I never figured he was much man, but I can't believe he's that bad. I'll take what Celia will give me and then I'll sashay out of town . . . which same will make you happy, I guess."

Her grip on his arms tightened. "Morgan, did you know that Dick was trying to take Molly away from you all the time you were engaged to her?"

"Well, yes, I figured that was what. . . ."

"And did you know he was the cause of Molly's giving

73

your ring back and that they're married now?"

The news jolted the breath out of him. He said after a long silence: "No, I didn't know that."

"Come to the house with me, Morgan," she said. "My mother's dead and I live alone. You'll be safe. I'll take care of you and hide you and I'll tell you a few things you need to know."

"I'll come after I see Lamar," he said, and turned to the door.

She stamped her foot. "Oh, you are a stubborn man. You always were. You haven't changed one bit. I'm going to get the sheriff. He's the only one who might keep Dick Lamar honest, but I'm not so sure he can."

She whirled away, and ran down the alley. He stared at her back until she disappeared in the twilight. For just a moment he wondered if he should have done what she said, then he shrugged. He could think of some men he ought to be afraid of, but Dick Lamar was not one of them.

He opened the door and walked along the hall past the door of Lamar's private office and went on into the bank. Then he found himself looking into the muzzle of Dick Lamar's gun.

The banker said: "Welcome back, sucker."

II

Sheriff Ed Smith climbed the stairs to Judge Alcorn's office above the bank. He was uneasy, and short-tempered because of it. The uneasiness stemmed from the fact that he didn't know what was going to happen, but he was dead sure that *something* was going to happen—something bad.

Plant enough whirlwind seed and sooner or later someone was going to reap it. There had been plenty of whirlwind seed planted in Twin Rocks basin, and Ed figured he was the most likely candidate to do the reaping.

The judge's door was open and Ed went in without knocking. Sam Colter, the hotel owner, and Baldy Miles, who ran the Mercantile, were already there. They were the town fathers who, along with Judge Alcorn, had run things as long as Ed could remember. That is, the three men had run things in accordance with the way old Abe Dill had wanted them run, and as long as Abe had been alive the relationship had worked very well. Now, with Buck Armand running the Rafter D, everything was different.

The men in the room nodded and said, "Howdy." The judge motioned to a chair and pushed a box of cigars at Ed. The three men were old; Ed Smith was of the following generation. He had a wife he loved and three children in whom he took inordinate pride. Because of them, he did not have the slightest desire to get himself killed.

No one said anything for a moment as Ed took a cigar and bit off the end. He fumbled in a vest pocket for a match, thinking that this situation reminded him of the saying about wars: the old men started them and the young men fought them. He didn't consider himself a young man at thirty-five, but he was still the right age to do the fighting and the dying. The other men weren't.

When Ed had his cigar going, the judge said: "I asked you men to come here to talk things over because I see some problems developing I'd like to get solved before they blow up in our faces."

"In case you're talking about the Rafter D," Baldy Miles said, "they owe me over two thousand dollars for supplies. Asking 'em for it is like spitting into a hard wind. I'd like to cut 'em off, but I'm afraid to. Buck Armand is the meanest bastard I ever seen."

Sam Colter laughed softly. "And we used to think old Abe was a mean one. At least you knew how you stood with him, but you never know how you stand with Armand or what he'll do."

"He wants something for nothing all the time," Miles grumbled. "That's one thing you always know about him."

"And he's pretty damned sure we're gonna give it to him," Colter added.

"So far you have," Ed said.

Miles and Colter got red in the face. Ed told himself he shouldn't have said it, but the truth was he couldn't stand up against the Rafter D by himself and he'd never had any help from the Twin Rocks businessmen. If Miles and Colter got sore about what he'd just said, he'd tell them a few of the facts of life.

They didn't say anything, but it was plain they hadn't liked what he'd said. They stared at the floor a while as the alarm clock on the judge's desk ticked off the seconds, then Alcorn said: "I've given in to Armand, too, Ed. I ain't proud of it, but I've done it, and I figure you have, too. You're afraid to arrest a Rafter D man. If you did arrest one of 'em, I'd be afraid to sentence him. Now it's got clean out of hand. Either

76

we do what we know damned well we should have done a long time ago or we resign and let somebody else enforce the law and handle the court."

"If you two resign," Miles said, "the rest of us might as well walk out of the basin and let Buck Armand have everything."

"I reckon you're saying the same thing the judge just said." Ed nodded at Miles. "I agree. It's time we all took a stand."

He paused, thinking again of his wife and children. He guessed he hadn't thought of much else the last few days. For a moment he wished he hadn't said what he had, then he saw the pleasure that washed across the judge's wrinkled face and he was glad he had said it, after all.

"Then we'll hang and rattle," the judge said. "There's two things that pushed me into calling this gab session. One is Armand's proposition to all the small ranchers that they've got to throw in with the Rafter D this fall when he drives to the railroad. On the face of it I guess it looks good. It'll save money and work all around, but Armand made it a have-to deal. I don't like that."

"You figure Armand will make some money for himself out of it?" Ed asked.

"I dunno," Alcorn admitted, "but it ain't like him to make an offer like that if he ain't feathering his own nest."

"He can overcharge the small fry for handling their stock," Ed said thoughtfully.

"He might grab the cars for his Rafter D steers and let the rest of 'em whistle," Miles said. "Seems like there's always a shortage of cars."

"Why, hell, he may just come right out and steal 'em," Colter said. "He's too big for his britches. He figures he's big enough to make it stick."

"All right, there you are," the judge said. "It's my guess he'll do one or maybe all of those things. The second item that worries me is more important because it can happen any day, while the roundup is two months off. What will happen if Morgan Dill rides into the basin?"

"Nobody knows where he is," Miles said, surprised.

"It don't make no difference where he is," the judge said. "I've got a hunch he'll be riding in any day. You see, old Abe always favored Celia as I reckon everybody knows, so his will put everything in her hands until Morgan was twenty-five. Well, his birthday is two days from right now."

"Armand will kill him," Ed muttered.

No one said anything for several seconds. They sat considering what Ed had just said. Finally Miles nodded his head. "He might at that. He's a killer. I don't figure Celia can stop him."

"I've been thinking along that same line," Alcorn said, "only it struck me that Armand might figure out a way to lure Morgan back into the basin just so he can kill him. Maybe there's no hurry for him to murder Morgan because the spread would all go to Celia if Morgan's dead. It's just that it would be a little neater and easier to handle if it happens before Morgan's birthday. At least, that's the way it seems to me."

"He always hated Morg," Ed said. "I saw a few cases of it when Abe was alive and Armand was rodding the Rafter D. It's my opinion that the will leaving control of the spread to Celia had more to do with Morg leaving the basin than Molly Runyan giving him his ring back."

"I wouldn't be surprised," Alcorn said.

"I don't savvy this," Colter said. "Morgan Dill's got to look out for his own hide. Why are *we* concerned about it?"

"Because I have always liked Morgan," Ed said sharply. "I

don't want to see him murdered if I can help it."

"There's another thing, too, Ed," Alcorn said. "I always figured Morgan was wild, but that was just the kid in him. He'll grow up, and, when he does, he'll be a good man. If *he* was running the Rafter D, we wouldn't have no trouble. On the other hand, if he's killed and we can prove Armand did it, which I figure we can unless Armand's smarter'n I think he is, and Ed goes out to arrest him, there'll be all hell to pay."

"Yeah," Ed said, feeling sick as he thought about it. "I might just shoot myself before I rode out there with Tully. The two of us would get shot, so we might as well save ourselves the ride."

"I still don't see what you're driving at, Judge," Colter said.

"It's time I laid it out," Alcorn said. "How much does the Rafter D owe you?"

"About two hundred and fifty for rooms and meals and drinks," Colter said.

"The way I see it," Alcorn said, "Armand never intends to pay it any more than he intends to pay Baldy. It boils down to a matter of extortion, with Buck Armand's thinking he's got everybody buffaloed to the place where he can keep getting everything free. Now I want you two"—he nodded at Colter and Miles—"to notify Armand that you'll sue if they don't pay immediately. I'll ride out to the Rafter D and deliver our message. If there's trouble, I'll be the one to get it."

"I'll ride with you," Ed said.

He wondered what his wife would say when he told her what he'd volunteered to do. Playing safe had become a habit, and he wasn't proud of his record any more than the judge was proud of his. Better not tell Mary what he was going to do, he thought. Not till he got back, if he did.

"I'll write that letter first thing in the morning," Miles said.

Colter nodded. "So will I. I ain't sure it's a smart thing to do, but I guess we've all reached the place where we don't like ourselves much. It's like we've been saying. We've got to take a stand."

"One more thing," Alcorn said. "I ain't sure it's got anything to do with Armand or not, or with Morgan. I'm thinking about Dick Lamar. If the gossip about his gambling is true, the bank may be in bad shape. I'd hate to think what will happen to the basin if the bank has to close its doors."

Ed rose and dropped his cigar butt into the spittoon. "Why don't you ask Dick about it?"

"I have," Alcorn said, "but he denies doing any more gambling than any of us do. He claims the bank's as solid as the Twin Rocks themselves."

"There's talk about it not being solid," Colter said. "We hear it in the hotel bar. It's got to the place where all it'll take is for someone to yell . . . 'Fire' . . . and we'll have a run on the bank."

"I have been thinking," Alcorn said, "that, if you two could get your money out of the Rafter D, and if we can borrow enough in Grand Junction, which I think we can, we'd do well to make Lamar an offer. I think he'd be glad to sell."

"We'd never raise that kind of money," Colter said, "though I've got to admit that we need a solid bank in Twin Rocks."

"This ain't none of my concern," Ed said, "so I'll get along home. Mary's been expecting me for an hour."

As he turned toward the door, the thought occurred to him that the whole conversation had been a waste of time. It was a matter of locking the barn after the horse was stolen.

They should have stopped Buck Armand as soon as he started throwing his weight around right after old Abe Dill died. Now it was probably too late, and all he and the judge would do, if they rode out to the Rafter D, would be to get themselves killed.

He stopped halfway to the door. Someone was pounding up the stairs from the street. A moment later Johnny Bedlow rushed into the room, out of breath. It took him a while to get his breath again, then he blurted: "Morgan Dill's in town. I just seen him." He swallowed and hurried on: "Buck Armand and a couple of his tough hands were in the shop getting their hair cut the other day. Armand got to talking about how ornery Morg always was to Celia. He said if Morg ever showed up in town, he'd kill him."

Ed wheeled to look at the judge, who was staring blankly at Johnny Bedlow. For several seconds there was absolute silence except for the hammering of the alarm clock. Then Alcorn said heavily: "He was just paving the way. What he'll really kill Morgan for is to keep him from claiming his half of the Rafter D."

"You've got to do something, Ed," Bedlow said. "Morg was my friend. That stinking bastard of a Buck Armand will do just what he says."

"If Morg will stay out of town . . . ," Ed began.

"But he ain't gonna do no such thing," Bedlow broke in. "You know that. He ain't the kind to run from nobody."

"Where'd you see him?" Ed asked.

"He was watering his horse in front of the Mercantile," Bedlow answered. "He said howdy and wanted to shake hands. All I could think of was Armand saying he'd kill him. I knew it wouldn't do no good to tell Morg to go hide, so I went to the courthouse to find you, and Tully told me you was here."

81

Again there was silence except for the alarm clock. Slowly Ed turned from Johnny Bedlow to face the judge. He asked: "How do you keep a man from being murdered?"

"You wait," Alcorn said. "You can't arrest a man just for what he says he's going to do."

"Yeah," Ed said gloomily, "and that'll do Morg a hell of a lot of good, won't it . . . arresting Armand after he's killed Morg?"

III

For a long moment Morgan stood staring at the banker, not moving a muscle. This was incredible. It simply made no sense. Dick Lamar had sent for him and then met him with a gun in his hand! Allowing for the fact that he had never liked Lamar and Lamar had never liked him, it still made no sense.

"What's the matter with you?" Morgan demanded. "And why am I a sucker? You wrote me that Celia was ready to make me an offer. You asked me to come to see you, and I did. What's the gun for?"

Lamar rose, the gun still lined on Morgan's chest. "The gun is to make sure you do what I tell you to," Lamar said. "You're a sucker for believing you'd get a good deal from Celia. I'm looking out for her interest, not yours."

Lamar motioned to a sheet of paper on the desk. Beside it was a pen and a bottle of ink. A canvas sack with the words, **Twin Rocks State Bank**, was there, too.

"I've got a right to know your intentions," Morgan said. "Do you intend to kill me?"

"Buck Armand would prefer it that way," Lamar said, "but I'm not one to take chances. I might have a hard time convincing the sheriff I had killed you in self-defense, so I don't intend to if I can help it, but I will if you don't do exactly what I tell you. I'm reasonably sure I could make it stick by telling Ed Smith you were holding me up and aiming to clean out the safe, but there is a slim chance he wouldn't believe me, so I'd rather play it safe."

Morgan's hands fisted at his sides and opened and closed again. With the exception of Buck Armand, he had never seen a man he could hate as wholeheartedly as he could hate Dick

Lamar. He told himself he should have listened to Jean. He had thought he had nothing to fear from Lamar, but he'd been dead wrong.

"All right, Lamar," Morgan said. "You got me here promising that Celia was ready to make a deal for my share of the Rafter D. I don't want any part of the outfit. I want my money and I'll go out to Oregon and buy a spread."

"Good," Lamar said. "Very good. That's what Celia wants, too. Now on the desk you'll find an agreement. Sign it. Beside it is a sack of money that Celia left for me to give to you. Sign the agreement and take the money. It's that simple."

"Then why do you need the gun?"

"I was afraid you'd have second thoughts about giving up your right to half of the property," Lamar said. "I don't aim to let you change your mind. Buck and Celia have worked hard on the Rafter D after your pa died. They have no intention of giving up half of it to you."

Something was wrong, but at the moment Morgan couldn't see what it was. He could understand about Celia and her husband wanting to keep the spread they were living on, and he could also understand Buck Armand not wanting him around for the simple reason that they had never got along and there was no reason to think, with Morgan three years older than when he had left the basin, that they would get along any better now.

He stepped up to the desk and picked up the paper. The statement was short and to the point:

I, Morgan Dill, being of sound mind, and understanding what I am signing, of my own free will do surrender any rights I have to the Rafter D in favor of my sister Celia. In exchange I acknowledge the receipt of one thousand dollars ($1,000.00) in cash.

Signature:_____.

Witness: _____Richard Lamar._

So that was it. For $1,000 he'd give up his half of the Rafter D, which was worth at least $25,000. He stepped back, and shook his head.

"So, that's the deal Celia is offering," he said. "You crooked son-of-a-bitch. You called me here to offer me. . . ."

"Don't call me names, you idiot," Lamar said angrily. "It won't do you any good. Celia wants this settled before you're twenty-five. It'll be less trouble this way. We didn't have to give you anything, but we thought it would be better to let you have a thousand dollars. Now sign the paper and take your money and git."

Morgan didn't move. He studied Lamar, thinking that the man had not changed in looks or habits. He had the same narrow, sharp-featured face and thin-lipped mouth, the same muddy brown eyes that never seemed to hold any expression and certainly did not reflect the smile that came so readily to his lips. He was smiling now as if certain Morgan would do exactly what he told him to do.

"I think I'll go see Celia," Morgan said. "This deal with you smells like there's something mighty rotten around here. I don't know whether it's you or the deal I smell, but I guess Celia can tell me."

The ready smile faded. Lamar's face turned red. He said: "I guess I didn't make myself clear. You don't have any choice. You'll sign or I'll kill you and swear you were robbing me. The safe door is open in case you didn't notice. There are a few gold pieces on the floor that I'll say you dropped when you ran. I'll tell Ed Smith you threw a gun on me and made me unlock the safe, then you grabbed all the money you could handle and left. Or started to, but I got hold of my gun in time

85

to kill you before you left the bank."

Lamar's face was cold and utterly devoid of feeling. Morgan had never heard of the banker killing anybody, but he was sure he was capable of it. Morgan was as sure of that as he had ever been sure of anything. He probably could make it stick, too. Ed Smith was a good sheriff, and he'd have his suspicions, but he couldn't prove that Lamar had murdered Morgan Dill. He'd have to believe Lamar's story.

Still Morgan hesitated, telling himself he would have signed the paper if Celia had offered any kind of reasonable deal. He had not expected $25,000, but he had expected a hell of a lot more than $1,000.

"Maybe you've never pegged me for a killer," Lamar said. "I don't want to be, but I'm in one hell of a tight squeeze. Killing you will get me out of it. I don't have any choice, Dill. Now make up your mind because I won't wait any longer." He thumbed back the hammer. "Now."

Death was there in Dick Lamar's face, and Morgan could believe the man was as desperate as he said. Morgan took a long breath, deciding it was better to take the money and sign his name than to be murdered. He'd see Celia before he left the basin. As much as they had disliked each other, he had never known her to be as greedy and unfair as this.

He stepped up to the desk, pulled the cork from the bottle of ink, and signed his name on the paper after the word **Signature**. He dropped the pen and picked up the canvas sack. "Now am I free to go?"

"You're free and you're going fast," Lamar said. "I'll give you thirty seconds to fork your horse and ride, and then I'm running to the back and I'll shoot at you. If you're riding fast, I'll miss, but if you hang around hoping to get a chance to pull your gun, I'll kill you."

He would do it. Morgan sensed that he was as close to

death at that moment as he had ever been in his life. He wheeled and ran out of the room and along the hall. When he reached the alley door, he glanced back. Lamar was walking toward him, the cocked gun still in his hand. Morgan knew that if he had made a move for his gun as he was running down the hall, he'd have been a dead man by now.

He lunged through the door, wanting only to get away. Once he was out of range of Lamar's gun, he could start thinking about what he could do, but right now the only smart thing to do was to get out of Twin Rocks. He swung into the saddle and, digging in the steel, rocketed down the alley. He heard two shots, the bullets kicking up dirt ahead of him and to one side, then he heard Lamar yelling: "Help! The bank's been robbed. Help!"

Morgan was out of town before he fully comprehended what had happened. Lamar was going to claim he had robbed the bank. Why? There could be only one reason. Lamar had robbed his own bank and he had to have a patsy. Morgan Dill was it.

He started to pull his horse to a stop, thinking he'd go back and face Ed Smith and his deputy, Tully Bean, and tell them exactly what had happened. But he didn't. He kept on out of town, thinking that neither the sheriff nor his deputy would believe him.

He'd been out of town for three years, and he'd had a reputation as a hell-raiser when he had lived in Twin Rocks. Lamar had been here all the time; he was a banker, a solid citizen. Hell, no, there wasn't a chance he'd be believed. If he claimed he'd returned to sign a paper and receive $1,000 for his part of the Rafter D, they'd figure he was lying.

When the town was a mile behind him, he paused on the bank of Twin Rocks Creek and stepped out of the saddle. As he let his horse drink, he remembered what Jean Runyan had said. She was right. He just didn't savvy a slick schemer like Dick Lamar who dealt off the bottom of the deck. Morgan was used to having everything in the open. As for Lamar's having robbed his own bank—well, it had just never occurred to him that the man would do it.

Actually Lamar wasn't just robbing himself. He was also robbing his depositors. Morgan didn't know what was behind it or what the squeeze was Lamar had mentioned, but he'd have to close the bank. Maybe he'd go to men like Judge Alcorn and Sam Colter and the rest of the businessmen in Twin Rocks and ask them to raise enough capital to start another bank. He'd come out of it smelling like a rose and Morgan would go to prison, if they caught him.

Morgan wiped a hand across his sweaty face. He couldn't see much sense in doing anything but getting out of the basin. If he had any chance to clear himself, he'd go back and fight it out. Then the thought came to him that he hadn't had time to think it out, that he had been surprised and shocked by what had happened. He was sore, too, right down to his boot heels for being taken by Lamar the way he had.

He jammed the canvas sack into one of his saddlebags. Flattening out on the rocks beside the creek, he took a long drink, but the water failed to drown the butterflies in his stomach. He was a hunted man. He had no one to turn to except Jean Runyan, and he guessed there wasn't much she could do for him now.

No use to wait here. Ed Smith and Tully Bean and maybe a posse would be along soon, so he'd better make tracks. Somewhere up in the high peaks to the north he could hole up for a while until his horse was rested. Sooner or later hunger would drive him on over to the other side to find food.

He had a Winchester in the boot and plenty of shells for it, and his revolver. He knew this country. He'd hunted all over it when he was in his teens and early twenties with Johnny Bedlow and Tully Bean. He stepped into the saddle, thinking the next few days would be interesting. Johnny and Tully knew the country as well as he did, and they'd be after him.

He rode north, glancing at the great orange moon that seemed to be floating above the eastern hills like a giant balloon. For just a moment a memory pang shot through him. He had sat on the bank of Twin Rock Creek many a summer evening with Molly's head on his lap and watched the moon come up just as it was coming up now. Then he muttered to hell with it. She belonged to Dick Lamar. He guessed it served both of them right. They were made for each other.

It was not until then that Morgan realized a fork of this road took him right past the Rafter D, the same road he had traveled hundreds of times coming into town and going home. He told himself he'd see Celia, then he gave it up. He certainly didn't want to see Buck Armand. There would only be trouble, if he did, but maybe Armand wouldn't be home. He spent most of his time during the summer in the cow camps to the north. If Morgan could catch Celia and talk to her, he'd soon know whether the $1,000 he'd been given was what she aimed to pay for his share of the ranch, or whether it was Dick Lamar's notion to cheat him.

He wasn't even sure that blaming him for robbing the bank was Celia's idea. It didn't seem like her way of doing things any more than chiseling him out of his part of the ranch for $1,000 had seemed like her. She'd probably changed in three years, but not that much. Maybe, if Celia had cash at the ranch, she'd add something to the $1,000. She usually kept a good deal of money there, partly to pay the crew. It was worth a try, he decided. If he was leaving the basin for good, he'd better have all the money he could get his hands on or he wouldn't have enough to invest when he reached Oregon.

A short time later he turned right on the road that led up the long hill to the Rafter D buildings. He wondered if he would have to kill his brother-in-law if he was home. He'd be doing Celia a favor if he did, and, after being married to Buck Armand as long as she had, the chances were she'd agree with him.

IV

The men in Judge Alcorn's office heard two shots from somewhere below them. For a moment no one was sure where they came from, then Alcorn shouted: "The bank! Lamar's down there. He told me he'd be working late tonight."

Ed Smith was the first through the door and down the stairs, Johnny Bedlow a step behind. When Ed reached the street, Dick Lamar charged out of the bank, yelling: "The bank's been robbed!"

Ed stopped, staring at Lamar in the finger of lamplight that fell past him through the street door of the bank. Bedlow stopped beside him, the three older men reaching the street a moment later. Someone was pounding down the alley, but still Ed stood motionlessly, staring at the banker.

"What's the matter with you, Sheriff?" Lamar shouted. "The safe was just cleaned out. You heard him riding away. Why aren't you chasing him?"

Under any other set of circumstances that was exactly what he would have done, but he was remembering the conversation about Lamar in Judge Alcorn's office. He had despised the man as long as he had known him. Lamar always reminded him of the garter snakes he had played with as a boy, squirming and twisting and a little too slick. Now, watching Lamar's flushed, narrow face, Ed asked himself why the banker couldn't get his work done in the daytime. Why was he working this late when he had never done it before?

"Who was it?" the judge asked.

After what Johnny Bedlow had said about seeing Morgan Dill in town, Ed figured he knew who Lamar would name. He

91

guessed that Johnny and the rest would think the same thing. Now, still watching Lamar closely, he thought the banker was more squirmy than ever. He looked as guilty as hell, then Ed told himself his imagination was working overtime. He liked Morgan Dill and he detested Dick Lamar. After serving ten years as a lawman, he was still making personal judgments, and that could get him into a pile of trouble.

Lamar took a long time answering. He looked at Ed, then at the judge, the corners of his mouth working nervously. Finally he said: "Morgan Dill."

Ed went past Lamar into the bank, Johnny Bedlow following. The door of the safe was open and this seemed queer, too. Lamar should have shut and locked it long before this. Ed guessed that Morgan Dill, if it had been Morgan, had been in too big a hurry to pick up the money he had dropped.

Lamar was there, then. His face was pale and the pulse in his forehead was pounding as if it were about to break through. He was scared, Ed saw, but if it had really happened, he had a right to be scared.

"Tell us about it," the judge said.

"It won't do any good," Lamar said in a high-pitched voice. "The sheriff just stands there, staring at me. A lot of folks are sure mistaken about him. They say he's a good sheriff."

"Go ahead and tell me what happened," Alcorn said. "Don't pay any attention to the sheriff."

Lamar swallowed. "I was sitting there at my desk. I'd had a busy day and I hadn't found time to clean everything up. I was almost done when young Dill walked in from the alley. He threw a gun on me and said he was taking all the cash I had. He did, too, except for what he spilled." The banker pointed to the coins on the floor, then jabbed a forefinger at Alcorn. "I thought he was going to kill me. He threatened to."

"How much did he get?" Alcorn asked.

"I don't know for sure," Lamar answered. "It'd be around ten thousand. I always keep that much cash on hand in case of an emergency of some kind."

Ed turned to the door, jerking his head at Alcorn. He said in a low tone: "Come on outside, Judge."

Tears began running down Lamar's cheeks. "Damn you, Smith!" he screamed in a shrill tone. "The longer you wait, the farther away he's getting. Aren't you even going to try to catch him?"

Ed stalked out of the bank, not answering. He waited on the sidewalk. When the judge joined him, he was irritated by Ed's behavior and showed it. Alcorn said: "I never saw you act this way, Ed. What's the matter with you?"

"A lot," Ed said. "A whole lot. This stinks to high heaven, Judge. Morgan Dill never robbed the bank."

Alcorn scowled and pulled at a tip of his white mustache. He asked: "How'd you figure that out?"

"Several things point that way," Ed said, "though I probably wouldn't have thought of it if we hadn't been talking about Lamar in your office."

"All right," Alcorn said. "What are they?"

"In the first place," Ed answered, "I can't see Morgan Dill robbing a bank, any bank, least of all coming home and robbing this one. In the second place, Lamar didn't have a busy day. I was in the bank twice and I walked past it several times and I never seen anyone in there except Lamar. In the third place, I knew Morgan Dill pretty well when he lived here, and I've talked to Tully about him. Tully and him and Johnny Bedlow used to run around together. He's not a man to threaten anybody, and then walk off and not do anything."

Alcorn was still pulling at his mustache and staring

thoughtfully at Ed. "I've been thinking some of the same things, but regardless of our suspicions the fact remains that Morgan was here and somebody was riding hell-for-leather getting out of town just now. That might have been Morgan. I want you to bring him in."

"He'll be a hard man to take," Ed said sourly. "It ain't that I'm afraid to tackle a hard man. I've done it plenty of times, but I figure Morg's not guilty, and I also figure he won't know I think that. I don't like the notion of killing or getting killed by an innocent man while the guilty one is sitting here grinning from ear to ear."

Alcorn nodded. "I know how you feel, but I need to talk to Morgan. About the Rafter D, for one thing. I also want to know his side of the story Lamar tells. It's a mighty funny business. I reckon the same idea occurred to you that I had. Lamar may have been stealing gradual-like, all this time, and, when he got down to cases, he figured out a way to get Morgan in here so he'd be blamed."

"That's about the size of it," Ed agreed, "but I sure can't see why Morg would show up here in the bank. Remember that Lamar married Molly Runyan, and, if a man was ever in love, Morg was in love with Molly."

"Which might be the reason he robbed Lamar's bank," Alcorn said. "Just to get even."

"Hell, he didn't do it," Ed said doggedly. "I figure Lamar must have put some kind of bait that fetched him to Twin Rocks, though I can't make a guess what it was."

"Well, go bring him in," Alcorn said. "We'll see."

Ed hesitated, not liking any part of it. He said: "I'll never find him. He knows the high country like the palm of his hand, and that's where he's headed."

"You've got to try," Alcorn said impatiently. "With Lamar swearing Morgan done it, you've got to go after him or

Lamar's long tongue will brand you from one side of the basin to the other."

"All right," Ed said, "but I'm going home and get something to eat first. I'll take Tully along, Johnny Bedlow, too."

Ed waited until Johnny Bedlow came out of the bank with Sam Colter, Baldy Miles remaining behind to talk to Lamar. Ed said: "Johnny, I want you to go with me and Tully. You know Morgan's habits as well as Tully does. Likewise, you know the country north of here."

Johnny shook his head. He said uneasily: "I don't want to go after Morg. I might have to shoot him and I always figured he was my friend."

"Damn it," Ed said harshly, "I don't want to go, neither. You go get Tully. Pick up a quick meal, both of you. I'll meet you with the horses at the jail in half an hour."

He wheeled and walked away, hoping they wouldn't catch up with Morgan Dill. He'd rather stay here in Twin Rocks and keep an eye on Dick Lamar, but Judge Alcorn had said to bring Morgan in. The smart thing was at least to pretend to do what the judge said.

V

Celia Armand sat staring through the window of her kitchen in the Rafter D ranch house. The moon was a full, round circle above the eastern hills and for one short moment she was aware of the beauty of it. She even imagined she could see a face in it, reminding her of a Halloween jack-o'-lantern.

She shrugged and, getting up from the table, walked to the stove and picked up the coffee pot. She filled her cup, and set the pot back on the stove. She had little time to think of any kind of beauty. Her life was filled with hard work and making money and scheming how to make more money, and fighting with her husband.

She often wondered why she had married Buck. She knew what he was before they were married. Her father had made him foreman a long time ago, but she didn't think old Abe had ever realized how completely ruthless Buck Armand was. She didn't know to this day whether her father had been killed by an accident or whether Buck had murdered him.

Old Abe and Buck had been hauling poles down from one of the peaks to the north and Abe's team had run away with him. He was thrown off the load of poles, his head had hit a rock, and Buck said he was dead by the time he got to him. Maybe it had been that way, but Buck could have hit the old man on the head with a rock and laid him on top of the load of poles and egged the team into running away. The body could have been thrown off the wagon and smashed up just the way it was whether it had been an accident or murder.

Celia knew one thing. Buck Armand was capable of murder. There were times when he looked at her speculatively, as if trying to think of some way to kill her so it would look as if it, too, had been an accident. That was the only way he could ever own the Rafter D. She was thirty years old, she was strong and healthy, and the odds were that she would outlive him.

She sipped her coffee, mentally admitting why she had married Buck. She had discovered a long time ago that she would never find a husband who loved her or who would marry her for what she was. No, any man would marry her because she owned half of the Rafter D; and, someday, if she were lucky, she might own all of it.

She was aware that she was hard to get along with. She was fat and ugly, with an upper lip that held more of a mustache than some men could raise. The answer was plain enough. She married Buck because she needed a man who would run the ranch the way she wanted it run. She had thought, too, that she could manage him. Well, she had been wrong about that. Dead wrong.

She had been just as ugly as a child as she was a woman. Her mother had been slender and frail and very pretty. Morgan, who had been a handsome child, had been her mother's favorite, so Celia had done everything she could to show her father that she loved *him,* and it had worked. After her mother died, she kept on proving to old Abe how much she loved him, although there had been times when she'd hated herself for being a hypocrite. But she had managed well, helping raise Morgan and doing the housework and always playing up to her father in such a manner that he let her have her way and usually asked her for advice on important matters.

As long as she lived, she would not forget that bitter afternoon when she had sat between Morgan and Buck in Judge Alcorn's office and heard the will being read. She had worked so hard to discredit Morgan with their father, playing up his recklessness and telling old Abe that Morgan would never grow up and be capable of running the Rafter D. It hadn't worked in the long run. She had supposed that Morgan would be cut out of the will, maybe getting "one dollar and various considerations" or something like that, with everything else coming to her. But the will had been plain enough. She got half and Morgan was to get half of the ranch when he was twenty-five. One thing saved Celia from going to pieces. She was given the operation of the ranch until Morgan's twenty-fifth birthday. It had been lucky for her that Morgan had quarreled with Molly Runyan and left the country.

Now the time had passed. In two days Morgan would be twenty-five, but neither she nor Buck had the slightest intention of letting him have any part of the ranch. He was coming back, and she wasn't sure yet it had been a smart scheme. Maybe it would backfire. Smart schemes did sometimes. The fear had been growing in her that, once Morgan was out of the way, Buck might find a method of getting rid of her and making it look like an accident.

She hated Morgan. It wasn't just that her mother used to make so much of the boy, then look at her with distaste and say: "You'd better marry the first man who asks you. You're a girl who'll never have much choice." No, it was more than that. Somehow Morgan seemed to have inherited all the good things. He was handsome, he was popular, and he always enjoyed himself whether it was a dance with the girls hanging all over him, or a 4th of July bucking contest which he usually won. It hadn't been fair, she told herself bitterly. She finally had found a husband, but she hated him, too.

Still, hating Morgan was not enough to make her want him murdered. It was what Buck aimed to do, if he had a chance. That was going too far. It was enough to buy him out for a small amount and get him to leave the basin.

98

She didn't know Buck was standing in the doorway watching her until she rose to get another cup of coffee. He stood, spraddle-legged, his pale blue eyes fixed on her, a faint smile on his meaty lips.

"How long have you been standing there?" she asked as she poured the coffee.

"Quite a while," he said. "You were a long ways off."

"A long ways," she agreed. "I was thinking. Don't kill Morgan."

"Who said anything about killing him?" Armand asked blandly. "I've said all the time I'll just beat hell out of him and put him on his horse and tell him to git."

"You don't have to say anything about it," she said wearily. "I know you better than you know yourself. As long as Morg's alive, you'll be worried about him coming back."

Armand's face turned red. "Well, I'd have a right to, wouldn't I? I don't aim to live the rest of my life worrying about him hiding on some rim or behind a tree and plugging me as soon as I get close enough."

"Don't do it," she said. "I'm warning you. The ranch is mine and it'll stay mine, but we don't have to murder my brother to get it." She paused, sensing the anger that was in him, and then she added: "I made a new will and left it with Judge Alcorn. It says you inherit nothing from me if I die by any kind of accident."

His face turned redder. "You think I'm going to kill you?"

"If you knew a sure way to do it and get away scot free, you would," she said. "A man gets used to murder, Buck. One, and then two, and finally three. That's what it would take to make a ranch worth fifty thousand dollars all yours. You were working a few years ago for thirty a month and beans. It wouldn't be bad, would it, Buck?"

"If you're thinking that of me," he said harshly, "you must

have the same notion about getting rid of me."

"Why should I get rid of you?" She shook her head. "No, I need you to run the outfit. You don't need me. It's that simple. I'm warning you again. Beat Morgan all you want to, but don't kill him, or I'll go to Ed Smith."

He made a step toward her, his head tipped forward on his bull neck, his great hands fisted at his sides. He stopped, breathing hard, then he said: "No use arguing about it. What I do with Morg depends on what he does. Maybe I won't have to kill him. Maybe the posse will do it for me."

"Or maybe he won't even stop here," Celia said. "I hope he don't."

"He'll stop, all right," Armand said with cold certainty. "He's got a thousand dollars in his pocket and he knows that, if he's satisfied and leaves with that, he'll never get any more."

"I wish I'd never agreed to your scheme in the first place," she said.

"Don't be a fool," he said harshly. "We don't have nothing to worry about. Dick Lamar is the one who's got his neck in a loop. Smith is no fool. The chances are he'll see through that fake hold-up and Lamar will wind up in the Canon City pen for about twenty years."

"You think Lamar will come out here tonight for that thousand he's giving Morgan?" Celia asked.

"Plus the extra four thousand he was to get from us for framing Morgan." Armand gave her a wicked grin. "Oh, he'll be here, all right, but if he pushes too hard, he'll get a dose of lead poisoning. All we have to say is that Lamar was trying to hold us responsible for what your outlaw brother done."

One murder led to another, she thought again. Now, staring at Armand's dark face, she told herself there wasn't any doubt about her father's death. It had not been an accident; it had been murder.

She opened her mouth to accuse him of old Abe's murder, but before she could say a word, he jerked his head at her. "He's coming," he said. "At least somebody's coming, and I'm guessing it's him."

She rose and followed him outside. She was glad she hadn't mentioned her father's death. She couldn't prove anything. All she would have done would be to hasten her own death.

VI

The Rafter D buildings lay at the end of the road that forked off from the county road that led into the high country to the north. Morgan had a strange feeling when he saw the familiar buildings in front of him. He had come home. It was a feeling he had never expected to have about the Rafter D.

Morgan pulled up beside the corral gate and sat his saddle, staring at the sprawling barn and outbuildings, and then at the two-story house farther up the slope. All of the buildings loomed up, tall and dark in the bright moonlight. Nothing about them had changed since he'd been a boy and had played in the mow of the barn and around the corrals, and yet in reality everything had changed.

A tall man left the bunkhouse and strode toward him, but Morgan didn't recognize him until he was less than ten feet away, then he saw it was Slim Turner, a cowhand who was about Morgan's age and had worked here since he was a kid.

"Howdy, Morgan," Turner said. "I didn't recognize you till I got up close."

"Howdy, Slim," Morgan said in a careful tone.

He had no idea how the cowboy would react to his presence. He had always liked the man and had every reason to think Slim liked him, but this was a different situation than it had been when both were riding for the Rafter D.

After a short pause, Morgan asked: "You the only one here?"

"Just me and the boss and Missus Armand," Turner answered. "I guess everybody's been looking for you to show up with your birthday only a day or so away."

Something had happened in the last few seconds as he

looked at this place he had once called home. His boyhood
had been happy enough as long as his mother was alive.
Maybe she had spoiled him as much as old Abe and Celia had
claimed. One thing was sure. After his mother died, he had
not been spoiled by anybody.

Now it struck him with sharp intensity that half of this
spread was rightfully his. He had made up his mind to accept
anything he could get from Celia and get to hell out of the
basin, but for some reason he reversed himself, knowing he
would not do anything of the sort. They would have to work
out some kind of arrangement with him, or divide the ranch.
If they tried to hold him to the paper he had signed in the
bank, he'd tell them he'd had no choice with Dick Lamar's
gun on him.

Slim Turner had come close to his buckskin and stood
looking up into his face as if trying to determine what was in
Morgan's mind. He said: "Was I you, I'd hightail out of here.
Everybody knows that half of the outfit belongs to you, but
owning it legal-like and getting possession are two different
things. Nobody except the boss knows what he's going to do,
but I figure I'd better warn you that he. . . ."

"Well! So the bad penny returns!" Buck Armand boomed.
"Celia and me thought it would happen about now."

Morgan stepped to the ground. He had not seen Armand
and Celia move out of the shadows around the house and
cross the yard to him. He wondered if Armand had heard
what Slim Turner was saying.

"Howdy, Buck." Morgan nodded at Celia who stood
behind her husband, as fat and broad-hipped as ever. He had
often wondered if her disposition was due to her physical ug-
liness. He added—"Howdy, Celia."—and waited.

Slim Turner moved away from him. Morgan stepped forward, watching Armand, who stood with his hands on his

hips, a squat, burly man who could kill with his fists. He was like a bulldog, Morgan thought, too stubborn to back up from a position he once had taken.

Celia did not return Morgan's greeting. He was unable to see her face clearly enough in the moonlight to make out what she was thinking and feeling. Suddenly she burst out: "Damn it, Morgan, why did you have to come back?"

Funny how a man changes direction, Morgan thought. A few minutes ago he would have said he had come back to sell his interest in the Rafter D for any reasonable amount she would give him, that he wanted more than the $1,000 he'd received from Lamar. Now, even though he had not forgotten that a posse would soon be after him and he had intended to high-tail it into the mountains, he knew he would do no such thing. He'd duck the posse and get back to town and he'd make Dick Lamar give back to him the agreement he'd signed, or make Lamar tell the sheriff the truth.

"I guess it's no secret why I came back, Sis," he said. "I always thought sisters kissed a brother when he'd been gone for three years."

"I haven't kissed you since you were a baby," Celia snapped. "You never wanted no kiss from me before, so I don't figure you want it now any more than I want to give you one. Now, why did you come back? If you think I'm going to give you more than five thousand for your share of the Rafter D. . . ."

"Five thousand? All I got was one." Morgan shrugged. "Anyhow, I changed by mind. I want my half of the Rafter D, not the money. What's more, I want an accounting of what's happened since I left, and a check for the half of the profit that's mine. After that, we'll decide whether we split down the middle, or if we can work it together. Personally I don't figure I could work anything with Buck."

"That's right," Armand said. "You couldn't work anything with me and we ain't aiming to give up half of the ranch. It's a good spread the way it is. Cut it in two and you'd have two hardscrabble outfits with neither one of us making a living on it. It won't do, boy."

Fury soared through Morgan. Armand was older than he was, but that did not give him the right to call him "boy" in that condescending tone. Morgan clenched his fists and thought of all the years he'd worked as a cowhand and had taken the dirty end of the stick.

"I own half of this spread," Morgan said. "I aim to get it."

"I tell you what we'll do," Armand said. "We'll give you another dollar for your share of the layout." He threw a silver dollar at Morgan that fell into the dust in front of him. "Now git on your horse and ride out of the basin."

"You heard the will read," Morgan said. "I aim to get my half if I have to go to the sheriff and Judge Alcorn to get it."

"Won't do you no good," Armand said. "You're the same damned punk kid you always were. You'll never change. You ride off and let us run the outfit and work our tails off, then you come back as big as life and claim your half. Well, sir, you won't get it."

He was bound to make a fight out of it, Morgan thought. It was more than trouble; it would be the kind of fight that would maim a man or kill him. He saw it in the challenging way Armand faced him. He heard it in the man's overbearing tone of voice.

Armand was wearing a gun. For a moment Morgan considered telling him to draw, that they might just as well settle their quarrel for good. Morgan didn't. He hoped it wouldn't come to that. He wasn't afraid of Armand's fists or his gun, and he wanted Armand to know it.

"If that's the way you're gonna perform, I'll get back to

town and find the sheriff," Morgan said. "I'll see the judge, too. There must be some law in this basin that ain't Rafter D law."

"You ain't going anywhere," Armand said. "I've wanted to teach you a lesson for a long time. I might as well do it now. When I get done, you'll wish you'd picked up your dollar and vamoosed."

He started toward Morgan, his big head tipped forward, his hands fisted in front of him. For just a short instant of time Morgan wondered if he had made a mistake. He had seen Armand fight; he had seen him smash more than one Rafter D hand who had been insubordinate or had done something so stupid that it had cost the ranch money. Armand fought in bull-like rushes, willing to take the hardest punch a man could give him in order that he could land one of his bone-smashing blows. Once he had his opponent down, he would give him the toe of his boot. More than one cowpuncher had been so crippled he had never been able to ride for a living again.

This wouldn't happen to him, Morgan told himself. He said: "Take off your gun belt, Buck."

Morgan unbuckled his gun belt and, turning, draped it across his saddle. Armand paused, scowling as if surprised, then he shrugged, jerked off his gun belt, and tossed it toward the barn. He came on again, his hands fisted. This time he hurried as if wanting to get the fight over with.

VII

Ed Smith had not walked ten steps after he left Judge Alcorn and Johnny Bedlow in front of the bank until he heard a woman call: "Sheriff! I want to see you, Sheriff."

He turned, irritated as he wondered what else had gone wrong tonight. Then he saw it was Jean Runyan and the irritation left him. She was a very pretty girl, decent and even-tempered, and as different from her sister Molly as two girls could be. He was often irritated with Molly, but never with Jean.

"Come ahead and see me," Ed said when she reached him. "I'm not hard to see."

"You were tonight," she said. "I've been all over town looking for you." She paused for breath, and added: "I couldn't find Tully, either."

"I left Tully in the courthouse," he said. "He must have gone home for supper. The judge called me over to his office for a palaver. What's wrong?"

Instead of answering his question, she asked: "What was the shooting about?"

He was silent a moment, wondering how much she knew about what happened. She was Dick Lamar's sister-in-law, but it was doubtful he would have told her what he was up to, if he was up to something. Finally he said: "Dick claims that Morgan Dill robbed the bank this evening and he shot at him."

"He's a stinking liar!" she cried. "Morgan didn't do anything of the kind. I saw him in the alley before he went into the bank. I told him not to go, that he didn't know how to handle a slippery crook like Dick Lamar."

"What makes you say Dick's a crook," Ed asked, "and why did Morgan go into the bank?"

"Doesn't everybody know Dick's a slippery crook?" she snapped. "I thought it was public knowledge."

"Maybe it is, at that," Ed admitted, "though I've never had any proof that he was. Now why did Morgan go into the bank?"

"I don't know," she said. "He told me Celia was going to buy his part of the Rafter D, but there's more to it than that. All I know for sure is that Dick sent for him. He read in the paper about Morgan's being in that fight in Steamboat Springs and getting jailed, so he wrote him to come to Twin Rocks."

"How did you happen to see him in the alley?"

"I knew he was coming," she said. "I don't really know much about it. I just overheard enough talk between Dick and Molly to know he'd sent for Morgan. It's some kind of a trap. It would be like Dick to rob his own bank and have Morgan on hand as a scapegoat."

That was exactly the way Ed had sized up the situation. He considered going back to the bank and asking Lamar why he had sent for Morgan, but it wouldn't do any good. Lamar would have some excuse, like saying Celia had authorized him to buy Morgan out. He was smart enough to have foreseen the question, and he'd have a ready answer.

"I've got to bring Morgan in," Ed said, "just to clear the record, since Dick's yelling about him doing it."

"You can't." Jean gripped both his arms. "Listen to me, Sheriff. Morgan is an independent kind of man. He won't let you put him in jail for something he didn't do. You know that. You'd feel the same way."

"I reckon I would," Ed answered, "but as sheriff I don't have no choice. At least I've got to try to bring him in, but I hope he's ten miles north of here by the time I start after him. Now you go on home. I'll let you know if anything happens."

She leaned forward to study his face in the moonlight. Apparently she believed him. She said—"All right, Ed."—and turned away.

He stood watching her until she disappeared down the street. He guessed that women were never very rational when it came to men. Jean must have seen a great deal of Morgan when he was engaged to Molly, but she had been a child then. Now she was a woman and there was no mistaking her feeling for Morgan Dill. Molly would have done better to have married Morgan than Dick Lamar, but it would have been worse for Morgan. Molly and Lamar seemed to have brought out the worst in each other. It was no secret that they fought like two alley cats.

Shrugging, Ed turned and went on toward his house, thinking that Molly's and Lamar's domestic problems were none of his business, but Morgan Dill's problems were. He guessed that made Jean's problems his, too. Well, one thing was sure. He'd take his time getting to the jail and starting out with Tully Bean and Johnny Bedlow.

He had always taken pride in being a good lawman; he had never held back when it came to risking his life going after a wanted man. Neither had Tully Bean, but this was a different proposition. Still, Judge Alcorn could make or break a man in Twin Rocks basin, and he'd said loudly and clearly to bring Morgan in.

Alcorn had a point, all right, with Dick Lamar accusing Morgan of the robbery. Ed didn't have the slightest doubt about Morgan's innocence or Lamar's guilt, particularly now that he knew Lamar had sent for Morgan. If he brought Morgan in and had his story about what had happened, he might be able to break Lamar down and get the truth out of him. Still, bringing a man like Morgan in was more than Ed could face. He couldn't shoot Morgan, if it came to that, but Morgan could sure as hell shoot him and he probably would.

When he reached the house, he found his wife and children finishing supper. He had a boy of six and two girls, four and three. When they saw him, they jumped down from their chairs and piled all over him, hugging and kissing him and getting grape jelly on his face.

His wife pulled the children off him and ordered them outside to play a few minutes before going to bed. When they were out of the house, she faced Ed, her hands on her hips, her lips drawn tightly against her teeth as they always were when she was angry.

"Well, Mister Sheriff," she said through tight lips, "you promised you would get home early. We held supper until it was practically spoiled. The children were so hungry I had to let them eat. Now it's cold for you."

He sensed that she was close to tears. He went to her and hugged her, then he said: "I'm sorry, Mary. I didn't have any way to let you know. The judge called me into his office along with Sam Colter and Baldy Miles, and, while we were there, the bank was robbed. Lamar claimed Morgan Dill did it. Now I've got to go after Morgan and I sure don't want to do it."

"I'm sorry, Ed," she said contritely. "I should have known it was something important. Sit down. I'll pour your coffee. At least it's still hot."

He pumped a basin of water and washed, then sat down at the table and began to eat. For a moment Mary stood watching him as if disgusted with herself for what she had said to him, then she shook her head.

"Something's wrong, isn't there?" she asked. "You don't think Morgan did it?"

"That's right," he said. "I wouldn't go, except that Alcorn said to bring him in. He ain't my boss, but if I want to get reëlected, I'd better do what he says."

"Is it so important to get reëlected?" she asked.

"Yes, it is," he said. "I knew how important it was as soon as I got home. A wife and three kids to feed! I can't go back to punching cows and that's all I know except packing a star."

"There must be other ways of making a living," she said. "Don't do anything you think is wrong just because you want to hold your job to feed us."

He kept on eating, not saying anything. Talk was cheap, he thought bitterly. He had seen more than one family starved into leaving the basin. The men weren't lazy. There simply were no jobs that paid a man enough to keep a family, not unless you had a little money of your own to invest in a business, and even then you couldn't be sure how it would work out.

No, he wasn't going to back out of what Judge Alcorn would say was his duty. The sheriff's salary was not great but they made out and even had a small savings account. He thought about Dick Lamar, who had inherited the bank from his father and had never done a day's work in his life. Lamar could be a crook and get away with it, but not Ed Smith.

He rose, when he finished, thinking that all he could do if he did catch up with Morgan was to play it safe and easy. That might be a little difficult because Morgan would be as dangerous as a treed cougar.

"I don't understand about the Dill boy," Mary said. "He's been gone a long time, hasn't he?"

Ed nodded. "Just got into town tonight, I guess. I don't know what did happen at the bank. All we have is Lamar's story."

"But Morgan Dill was always a troublemaker, wasn't he?"

111

"No, not really a troublemaker," Ed said. "Just reckless. Always up to some orneriness, him and Tully and Johnny Bedlow. Tully's straightened out and I guess everybody likes Johnny. I figure Morgan would do the same if we give him enough time." He kissed Mary, then said: "Go on to bed. I don't know when I'll be back." He heard the children screaming in play from the front of the house, and added: "I'll go out through the back. Just tell them I had some work to do tonight."

He stopped in the back doorway and turned and looked at his wife. He was tempted to go back and kiss her again. She was younger than he was by five years, still slim and attractive of body after bearing his three children. He loved her more than he could ever tell her, and sometimes just the thought of getting killed and leaving her with nothing but the house and a few dollars in savings was more than he could stand. It was at times like that when he seriously considered not running for office again, but he knew more broken-down hungry cowpunchers who couldn't work—than he did dead sheriffs.

Quickly he turned and strode across the yard to the barn. He saddled his black gelding, and rode to the livery stable. He had taken more than the half hour he had told Johnny Bedlow to wait. Maybe Johnny had got tired and had gone home. Tully Bean would be waiting at the jail regardless of what Johnny did. He'd raise hell about going after Morgan, but he'd do it.

Ed saddled Tully's horse while the hostler saddled a livery animal for Johnny, then Ed left the stable leading the three horses. Tully and Johnny were waiting at the jail and both were cranky.

"I was just fixing to leave," Johnny said sullenly.

Tully said: "This is the damnedest thing I ever heard. Old Morg wouldn't rob no bank. If you ask me, it was that slick-

112

tongued Dick Lamar who robbed his own bank and blamed it on Morg."

"We've thought of that," Ed said. "It's one reason we're going after Morgan. We need to hear his story about what happened."

He didn't tell them how near he had come to not going after Morgan. One thought did give him a little comfort. Maybe Morgan didn't know he was being accused of bank robbery and wasn't really running. Perhaps they would find Morgan somewhere to the north, camped along the creek, and they could sit down and talk about it, and he'd come back to town and tell Judge Alcorn and the others. Then he could arrest Dick Lamar and get the truth out of him and release Morgan.

Ed grinned as he mounted and reined his black into the street, Johnny and Tully falling in behind him. He knew he was thinking plain hogwash, and he wondered how far a man's imagination would take him if he let it go.

A moment later the town was behind them, their shadows dark against the grass in the bright moonlight. They crossed the bridge spanning Twin Rocks Creek, the horses' hoofs striking the planks with pistol-like sharpness.

Ed stared north toward the sharp, granite peaks that raked the sky. He couldn't see them now because they were too far away to be seen in the moonlight, but he had been over the range and he knew how hard it was to get to the other side. There were passes, all right, but they were tough and steep. Morgan could make it, though. He knew the country and he wouldn't forget how it was in the three years he had been gone. It would be sheer hell to chase him over the range. Ed could think of many places up there where Morgan could hole up and cut all three of them down before they could find any protection.

As he thought about it, he told himself Morgan Dill wouldn't do that, and knew at once he could not make such a judgment. There was—and Ed had learned this lesson well—no way to tell what a man would do when he was pressed hard enough.

"What do you think he'll do, Tully?" Ed asked.

"He'll keep going," the deputy answered, "but I'm damned if I know which pass he'll take."

"Johnny?"

"Same here," Johnny Bedlow said. "He'll keep going, all right, but there's at least three passes he could use to go over the range and we've got no way of telling which one he'll take. I ain't sure we can follow his tracks, either, once he gets above timberline."

"Or what he'll do if we're right on his tail," Tully said. "I keep thinking about something, Ed. We don't know how much he's changed in three years. I've changed plenty since Morg left the basin. So has Johnny. Well, we don't know how much Morg's changed or in what direction. He may be a curly wolf by now for all we know."

"I've been thinking the same thing," Johnny said grimly. "He ain't gonna be the same happy-go-lucky, hell-raising kid we used to ride with. He's got plenty to be bitter about, with Molly throwing him over and Celia and Armand treating him the way they have."

What they were saying, Ed thought, without quite putting it into words was that the Morgan Dill they had known three years ago would not, or maybe could not have held the bank up, but the Morgan Dill who had returned might. Certainly he had not come back just for a visit with old friends. Ed sighed. As he thought about the rugged passes that were ahead of them, he told himself there was but a very slim chance they could follow Morgan's trail over the top. He was thankful for that.

VIII

Buck Armand charged at Morgan with the tough confidence of a man who had never been beaten in his life. Morgan did not back away; he saw Armand start his blow below his waistline and saw the big fist swing up straight for his head, a pile-driving blow that would have knocked him cold if it had landed. Morgan tipped his head to one side just enough so that Armand's fist barely missed. The momentum of his charge carried Armand on past Morgan who sledged him on the cheek as he went by, a wicked blow that would have knocked a lesser man down, but all it did to Armand was to drive a grunt out of him.

The big man wheeled ponderously and rushed again, this time with his arms spread. If he succeeded in catching Morgan in his powerful grip, Morgan knew that his ribs would be crushed. Again he waited, timing his move to the exact second, then he raised a knee. Armand was coming in, bent over, hoping to catch Morgan around the waist. Instead, Morgan's knee smashed him under his chin, snapping his teeth together in an audible *click*. He hit the ground and lay there for a moment before he reared up, shook his head, and struggled to his feet.

This time the Rafter D man came at Morgan more carefully, his fists cocked in front of his face. Morgan was taller by a good six inches and so had the advantage of a longer reach. He drove a straight right into Armand's face before Armand was close enough to hit him. The blow smashed Armand's nose and brought a rush of blood. Morgan whipped a left through to Armand's face before the big man could recover, working on the principle that the best defense is a slashing offense. This time he smashed Armand's lips against his teeth, bruising and cutting both of them.

Morgan knew he had hurt Armand, hurt him enough to make him more cautious, perhaps had hurt him enough to take some of the brutal power out of his blows. Now Morgan elected to stand and fight, weaving and ducking and taking more blows on his forearms than he did on his face or body. All the time he was using his right and occasionally his left to batter Armand's already bloody face.

Morgan was getting hit, but the blows lacked the knockout power that had been in the first ones. Morgan worked on his eyes, on his nose again, and then in a careless moment let Armand catch him with a roundhouse right to the jaw. He staggered back, the world tilting and turning in front of him. He had not thought Armand had that much strength left, a mistake that came close to beating him.

Now Morgan back-pedaled, making a circle as he held Armand off and looping blows until his head cleared. In spite of his longer reach, now and then Armand got a punch through to Morgan's body that hurt and it became an effort to breathe. Armand was clumsy and slow, but still there was enough power in his blows to hurt when he landed one.

Armand was almost out on his feet and fighting more from instinct than conscious direction, but Morgan was plagued by the nagging feeling that he wasn't going to last. It was like fighting a bear that kept coming and was always dangerous as long as he was on his feet. Morgan knew, then, he had to make the kill, that if he kept on this way, he was bound to lose in the end because of the superior animal strength that was in Buck Armand. He backed up, feinting with his left, and Armand took the bait, thinking Morgan was finished.

Once more the big man lunged at Morgan, a great fist swinging out in a roundhouse blow. Morgan ducked and drove in, and now Armand was wide open. Morgan caught him flush on the jaw with a wicked, turning fist that connected with the impact of a slamming club. It rocked Armand's head. For a moment he struggled to stay on his feet; he tried by the sheer power of will to drive another blow at Morgan's body, but his legs would not hold him, and he spilled forward on his face.

Armand was still conscious. His hands began searching on the ground for the gun he had dropped. As far as Morgan knew, the man had never been knocked off his feet before. He had no stomach for more, but there was little doubt about what he would do if he found his gun.

When Morgan realized what was in Armand's numbed mind, he wheeled to his horse and yanked at the holstered gun. He had it half out of leather when the sky fell on him. He went down at the side of his horse, the gun dropping back into the holster.

Morgan came to with a whacking headache. He lay on his back, staring at the sky. The moon was still up there, a fact that vaguely comforted him. He was wet. As he wiped his face and sucked air into his lungs, a man said: " 'Bout time you was coming around."

Morgan didn't recognize the voice for a few seconds, then he realized it was Slim Turner who had spoken to him. Apparently the cowboy had brought him around by throwing a bucket of water on him.

Morgan sat up slowly and put a hand to his head. He asked: "What hit me?"

"Missus Armand slugged you," Turner said. "She picked up a piece of limb or something. I guess she figured you was gonna drill Buck. You'd be worse off than you are if you'd shot him. He was trying to find his gun, and I guess he would have if I hadn't tossed it clean back to the corner of the barn.

117

Come on and get on your horse. When Armand comes out of the house, he'll have a gun. Git moving. I've helped you all I can. Armand will kill me if he finds out I've helped you this much."

Morgan got to his feet and staggered to his horse. He grabbed the saddle horn, his head hammering as if a dozen devils were using it for a drum. He stood there a moment, his eyes shut until the worst of the headache passed, then he pulled his gun belt off the saddle and buckled it around him. He raised a foot to the stirrup, and with a great effort swung into the saddle.

He rode toward the creek. Every step the horse took sent a slashing pain up through his head. He bent forward, hanging onto the horn and swaying in the saddle. He knew he couldn't ride, but he didn't dare stay in the open where Buck Armand could find him. One thing was as certain as death and taxes. As soon as Armand could sit his saddle, he'd start looking for Morgan.

It wasn't just that Buck Armand had been beaten for the first time in his life. It was more than that. He had built a reputation in the basin as a fighting man and now it was shattered; he had been humiliated before one of his cowhands and in front of his wife. He would never rest until he had repaid Morgan by killing him.

Morgan crossed the road and went on to the creek. He stepped down, again holding to the horn until most of the dizziness passed, then he led his buckskin through the willows to the bank. He let the reins drag and, kneeling, sloshed water onto his face. In time the headache would pass and he could defend himself, but he wasn't sure how much time he had.

He sat there, trying to arrange his thoughts, but he felt drained out as if every muscle in his body had been bruised and hammered until it ached like a throbbing tooth. It wasn't just the blow on the head that Celia had given him. Armand had hurt him more than he had realized. It was always that way in a fistfight. More blows were landed than a man was aware of at the time.

Presently his head cleared and he found that he could think. First, he'd remind Judge Alcorn of his claim to half the Rafter D and tell how he had been treated. He wasn't sure what had changed his mind, but he was very sure he was not pulling out and leaving all of the ranch in Celia's and Armand's hands. If they had been reasonable, he might have reversed himself again and sold his share of the ranch, but Armand had intended to kill him or maim him for life.

Then he remembered hearing Lamar yelling bank robbery. They would be hunting him, too—Smith and a posse. He wondered if they had ridden past while he was fighting with Buck Armand.

Again he realized how much he needed time to rest and regain his strength. The only place he could do that would be back in town in Jean Runyan's house. He remembered, too, that she had promised to tell him some things he needed to know.

Suddenly it came to him he was not thinking straight. He was putting things in the wrong order. Before he looked up Judge Alcorn and talked about his half of the ranch, he'd better clear himself of the bank robbery. The only way he could do that was to get hold of Dick Lamar. When he did, Lamar would tell the truth or he would be a dead man.

Morgan rose and turned to his horse, then he froze. Horses were coming upstream. It might be Ed Smith and his posse. Morgan couldn't risk being arrested and taken to jail now, not until he had beaten the truth out of Lamar. When it came right down to it, he wasn't going to jail at any time. He had been locked up only once in his life. He'd go crazy if he were jailed even for a few hours. That one time had been enough.

A few minutes later the riders came into sight. He had guessed right. The lead man was the sheriff. *Funny,* Morgan thought, *only three men after him. Not much of a posse.* When they were closer, he saw that the other two were Tully Bean and Johnny Bedlow.

He watched them rein up in the fork of the road. For a time they talked, but he was too far away to hear what they were saying. Tully Bean was motioning toward the mountains to the north, then he stepped out of the saddle and began studying the road.

Morgan drew his gun and waited. It was enough to make a man laugh, he told himself. Smith had picked the two men who knew him better than anybody else in the basin, the two men who had been his best friends.

Suddenly Tully got up off his knees and straightened as he turned to Smith. He said: "I can't make it out, Ed. You know, he could be hiding right under our noses."

Morgan lined his gun on Tully's chest, wondering if he could bring himself to shoot either Tully Bean or Johnny Bedlow if they decided to root him out. The three of them had raised a lot of hell together, then he reminded himself they were hunting him, hunting by that damned full moon overhead. If they found him, they'd shoot him for resisting arrest. Or, if he surrendered, they'd take him to jail. His lips squeezed together into a hard, bitter line. He knew then he could and would shoot either one or both if it came to that. He was not going to jail.

IX

Ed Smith rolled a cigarette, looking down at Tully Bean in the moonlight. He thought he knew what Tully was trying to tell him, that fresh hoof prints in the road indicated Morgan Dill was hiding in the willows. There was a good chance that he had his gun lined on one of them right now. Again the thought came to Ed that there was no way of knowing how much Morgan had changed in the three years he had been gone, but he had been a tough hand when he had lived in the basin. The chances were he had not softened any during these three years. Morgan Dill was not the kind of man who could stand being locked up in a jail. Tully Bean had said this about him more than once. He was like a wild animal that was penned up; he'd get sick and die. If that was true, and Ed had a hunch Tully knew what he was talking about, Morgan would shoot it out with anyone who tried to take him to jail.

Ed fired his cigarette and flipped the charred match away. He said, trying to keep his tone casual: "Get back on your horse, Tully. We'll take a sashay up to the Rafter D. Morgan might have taken a notion to see his sister."

"Sure," Tully said as if relieved. "That's just about what he done."

Tully mounted, and Ed led the way up the Rafter D road. A moment later Tully moved up beside Ed. He said: "He was down there in the willows, all right. I could feel my skin crawling. If you'd said we were gonna hunt for him, he'd have let go and some of us would have got hurt. It would have been like shooting fish in a barrel with the moon as bright as it is."

"Yeah, we'd have got hurt permanent-like," Johnny Bedlow added grimly. "It'd been you or me, Tully, or both.

Morg never was one to forgive a friend who turned on him."

"That's the way I was figuring," Tully agreed.

"Who knows what to do in a case like this?" Ed asked. "I sure don't. I'm still not sure he robbed the bank. Or if he did do it, I'd like to know why and just what did happen."

"Maybe we should have hollered at him," Johnny said. "If he was close enough to shoot us, he was close enough to holler at."

"No, he wouldn't have answered," Ed said, "unless he done it with a bullet." He paused, remembering how positive Tully was that Morgan was hiding along the creek, and the thought occurred to him that his deputy might have lied to give Morgan more time to get away. He asked: "What made you think he was down there, Tully?"

"I don't know that he was," Tully answered, "but it was pretty plain that somebody had ridden up the Rafter D road and then had come back and gone across the county road into the willows. Now, if he was headed out of the country like we figured he was, he'd have turned north there at the forks. Or gone back to town if he figured he still had business there."

"I don't see much sense in hiding in the willows," Johnny said. "Might have been somebody else who made them tracks."

"Sure, sure," Tully said irritably. "I told you I didn't know for sure, but who else has been riding around this time of night? Damn it, I know Morg. He'd plug us before he'd go to jail. I can tell you I didn't feel downright comfortable a while ago."

A moment later they rode into the yard of the Rafter D. Ed saw there were lights in the back of the house, then he heard Tully say softly: "Over yonder, Ed. In the corral."

He looked to his left. A man was saddling a horse, but he couldn't see who it was even in the moonlight. He swung left just as the man led his horse out of the corral and closed the gate. He saw then that the man was Slim Turner.

"Where you headed, Slim?" Ed asked as he reined up.

Turner stepped into the saddle, then sat there, staring at Ed. Tully rode forward on one side, Johnny Bedlow on the other, so that Turner was boxed in unless he wanted to bull his way through. If he had any such thought, he changed his mind when Ed dropped his hand to the butt of his gun. He said softly: "I won't ask you again, Slim."

"I'm going to Indian Springs if it's any of your damned business," Turner said sullenly.

"You seen Morgan Dill?"

"Yeah, I seen him."

"Where?"

"Here."

"Was he here very long?"

"No."

"How long?"

"How the hell do I know?" Turner snapped, exasperated. "I didn't time him."

Something was wrong, Ed thought. Whatever it was must be important or Turner wouldn't be acting this way. Normally he was a friendly and talkative man.

"Maybe you'd better come to town with us," Ed said. "I always find that a man talks better in jail or sitting in my office than he does when he's outside forking his horse."

"You can't do that," Turner said hotly. "The boss is sending me on an errand. He'll have my hide if I don't get it done."

"I'll have your hide if you don't talk, so take your choice," Ed said. "Now let's have it. What happened when Morgan showed up?"

Turner hesitated, his gaze turning to Tully, then Johnny

Bedlow. Apparently he decided there was no way out unless he talked, so he blurted: "We all knowed he was coming or guessed he was, seeing as half the Rafter D belongs to him, or will in a couple of days. That's why Armand's been keeping me here. Tonight Morgan rode in and got into a fight with Armand. He gave the boss a pretty good whipping and took a lot of punishment himself. After he knocked the boss down, Missus Armand knocked him cold with a club. He came around when I threw some water on him. He got back on his horse with a little help from me and rode off. I don't know where to, though."

So that was it, Ed thought. He had been hurt, hurt enough so that he didn't feel like riding. He had plenty of reason to hide out in the willows. Ed asked: "Why is Armand sending you to Indian Springs?"

"To get the crew," Turner said, meeting Ed's gaze with the arrogance that was typical of a Rafter D hand. "It figured that Morgan went back to town to get you and to tell the judge about what happened out here. The main thing is he took a whipping and he ain't aiming to let it go."

Fury swept through Ed. He said: "Didn't it ever occur to Armand that he's not the law in the basin?"

Tully snickered. "You ever hear of a notion like that coming into Buck Armand's head?"

"I didn't give the order," Turner said sullenly. "I just work for the Rafter D. You want some answers, go talk to Buck."

"All right, I will," Ed said, "but you tell the rest of the crew that I'll throw the whole outfit into jail if they try to stop the law from being enforced or to take the law into their own hands." As Turner started to ride away, Ed added: "You might remember that there's a good chance you'll be working for Morgan Dill when this is settled."

"No," Turner said, "he'll be a dead man. I've got nothing

124

against Morgan. I wish he'd get out of the basin and stay out. Nobody stands up to Armand and his wife and wins, and you know it."

Then Turner spurred his horse around Tully and rode downslope as if anxious to get away from Ed and his questions.

"Well," Tully said thoughtfully, "he's got a point. Now the time's come."

"What time?" Ed demanded.

"The time to see if Slim's right. Who does run the basin? Is it the sheriff's office or the Rafter D?"

Tully had needled Ed about this before and his question didn't help settle his anger now. Ed said: "Come on. Let's go see what Buck Armand's got to say. Might be we'll have to cut the Rafter D down to size and tonight's as good a time as any."

X

Morgan waited until Ed Smith and his men were well up the Rafter D road before he holstered his gun. He led his horse back to the road, stood motionlessly for a time beside the animal, one hand clutching the saddle horn, then his head cleared and he mounted, and rode slowly toward town.

When he reached the business block, he turned off Main Street and followed an alley to the back of the Runyan house. His head still ached, but he felt better than when he had left the willows. He turned his buckskin into the barn, tied him in a stall, and loosened the cinch, then stepped back into the alley.

He glanced at the sky and judged the time to be midnight or later. For a moment he thought about Dick Lamar and wondered if the banker would stay in town or pull out. If he were smart, he'd stay and bull it through, but Morgan figured him for a coward, and he doubted that the man had enough guts to stay after what had happened. Either way, Morgan knew he wasn't up to facing the man, and it would be stupid to tackle him until he was ready. He had maybe four hours until dawn and he'd better use some of that time to rest. Jean would see that he had a chance to sleep and probably eat supper. She was still up. At least there was a light in the house.

Quickly he crossed the yard to the back door, stepped up on the porch, and knocked. He heard footsteps cross the kitchen, then the door opened and Jean stood there, holding a lamp in her hand. She said: "I thought it would be you, Morgan. Come in."

He stepped inside. She looked at him and shook her head.

"What happened? You didn't get your face messed up doing what Dick wanted you to do."

"I had a fight with Buck Armand."

"I guess that was to be expected." She motioned to a chair at the table. "The water in the teakettle is hot. I'll clean your face up. I'll pour a cup of coffee for you, too. Have you had anything to eat?"

"Not for a long time." He tried to grin at her, but his lips wouldn't behave. "I feel like hell. Now that I stop to think about it, I'm hungry. I guess breakfast was the last time I et and that was before sunup. Maybe that's what's wrong with me."

"I wouldn't be surprised," she said.

She poured the coffee, then brought a bottle from the pantry and laced the coffee with whiskey. "Go ahead and drink," she said. "I'll see what I can do with your face and then I'll rustle something for you to eat." She stepped back and looked at him gravely. "You're a stubborn man, Morgan Dill. You're over your head when you start dealing with Dick Lamar. He can make a fox look like a fool."

Morgan sipped the coffee. As she brought a towel and a basin of hot water to the table, he said: "I ain't in any shape to argue with you."

She dropped one end of the towel into the basin of water, lifted it out, and squeezed it as dry as she could, then gently began to wipe the blood from his face. She examined each bruise and cut, then dabbed at them with the dry end of the towel, and finished by rubbing salve on them.

"Nothing very serious," she said. "Now I'll get you something to eat."

He drank the coffee and, closing his eyes, leaned back in his chair. His head still hurt and he had never felt so tired in his life. He was almost asleep when she said: "You'd better eat, Morgan. I'll talk while you're eating, then we'll decide what you're going to do."

"*We'll* decide?" He pulled his chair up to the table thinking that Jean was more like her sister than he had realized. Molly used to say things like that. "I might as well make it plain. I'll decide."

Jean smiled. "All right, you decide. I'm going to lock the house. Somebody, either the sheriff or Armand, might think you'd come here and walk right in."

She was gone for two or three minutes, then she returned and locked the back door, and pulled the blinds in the kitchen. She sat down across the table from him and studied him for a moment before she spoke.

"I said I'd talk," she said. "I had no intention of deciding anything for you. I was going to tell you some things you probably don't know. After you hear them, you can decide all you want to." She hesitated, then added: "I know how Molly was and is, even now that she's married to Dick. I've always said I'd never try to boss a man, you in particular."

She had brought several slices of roast beef to the table along with bread, butter, and a quarter of custard pie. She filled his coffee cup again and sat down. He watched her as he ate, thinking she wasn't much like Molly, after all. Jean didn't really look like her sister, not when he sat here and looked closely at her. Her hair was the same ebony black, so black that it held blue tints in the lamplight, her eyes were the same dark brown, and she was nearly the same size. The difference was in her expression. Molly had always been discontented and her face had showed it. Now that he thought about it, Morgan couldn't remember when she had been satisfied about anything. Jean was more straightforward, without any sign of being unhappy or expecting to be waited on and taken care of. Molly had always acted as if she were royalty, but

Jean made no pretense of being anything more than she was. Then Morgan noticed something that he had not thought of before. Molly had always looked older than she was, perhaps because of the crow's feet around her eyes, but Jean looked young and fresh and very attractive.

Suddenly Jean laughed. "I guess we've both changed, haven't we, Morgan? While you're looking me over and wondering if I've really grown up, I've been looking you over and wondering if you've changed. You were a harum-scarum kind of fellow when you left here, you and Tully Bean and Johnny Bedlow. Sure, I was just a kid, but I knew a lot about you. It always seemed to me you had a lot of fun."

"I did," he said, "but I haven't had much fun since I left the basin."

He went on eating, realizing that he hadn't really thought much about it, but he had had a lot of fun when he'd lived here. Molly was always ready to go any time he could take her, and a man couldn't have had better partners than Tully Bean and Johnny Bedlow. They were all for it any time he suggested any hell-raising.

Morgan hadn't had a girl since he'd broken up with Molly and he hadn't formed any real friendships with other men since he'd left the basin. Now, thinking about Tully and Johnny, he told himself it would have been hell if he'd been forced into shooting them up there on the creek. Well, the night wasn't over. They might get on his tail again before morning.

For some reason Jean seemed reluctant to start talking, but she remained seated across the table from him, her hands folded in front of her. As Morgan reached for the pie, she said: "This is going to hurt you and I hate to do it, but you'd better know it just in case you're still in love with Molly. She never loved you. She's been a calculating, selfish bitch as long

129

as I can remember. I ought to know. I used to get the short end of the stick time after time. That was when Ma was alive and the three of us lived here."

Morgan picked up the piece of pie from the dish and ate it with his fingers. He wasn't surprised by what Jean had said. He just hadn't ever admitted it to himself, but he'd known Molly pretty well, well enough to be sure that she was a person who made it a point to look out for herself first.

"She wanted to marry you as long as she thought you'd get at least half of the Rafter D," Jean went on. "At one time, before Celia married Buck Armand, I think Molly dreamed about you getting all of the ranch, but then it got to be common gossip in the basin that Celia would work it so you got nothing. Or at least you'd have nothing for three years and Molly was never one to wait. Dick began seeing her on the side and she encouraged him. You don't do much better than landing a banker for a husband, so she promised to marry Dick before she gave your ring back. Besides, she wouldn't have to work as hard if she married a banker."

Jean stopped as if wondering how he was taking it, then rose, and, going to the stove, picked up the coffee pot and brought it to the table and filled his cup. Morgan didn't say anything. He guessed that hearing this was the best medicine Jean could give him. He had never really got over being in love with Molly, although it had been a sort of festering sore in him because he had not understood why she had given the ring back. Now that he knew, the sore would heal. He didn't doubt what Jean told him. It was exactly the way Molly would operate.

Jean returned to her chair across the table from him. "One other thing you don't know is that Dick Lamar is broke and the bank is on the rocks. At least, there's a lot of talk along that line and Molly has hinted at it more than once. She feels

sorry for herself, I guess, and wants sympathy. Anyhow, that
was why I was so sure Dick was baiting a trap for you, though
I didn't know what it was. The thing with Molly is that she's
scared she's going to lose her home and her position in the
community as the banker's wife. Dick always has gambled a
good deal. Lately he's been doing more of it. I think he's been
stealing money from the bank and losing it at poker. It would
account for his accusing you of robbing the bank. It's one way
he can get into the clear."

Morgan picked up his cup and drank the rest of the coffee.
He was still tired, so tired he couldn't think straight. His head
didn't hurt as much as it had, but he felt as if he were glued to
his chair and lacked the energy to free himself. He rolled and
fired a cigarette, thinking he would ask Jean to let him sleep
for an hour, then he'd look Lamar up and he'd get the truth
out of him if he had to half kill him.

"I'm going to have to sleep a while, Jean," he said. "Wake
me in an hour and I'll get up and do what I have to do. I've
never killed a man, but I may kill Lamar."

"You can sleep here, of course." But she didn't get up.
Her eyes remained pinned on his face, a questioning expression in them. "Morgan, I keep wondering if this was all
Lamar's idea. Or did Molly think of having him rob the bank
and sending for you and making you the scapegoat?"

"I don't know who thought of that," he said, "but I guess I
asked for the whole business. You see, it wasn't just that
Lamar read about me being in the ruckus in Steamboat
Springs and knowing I was there because of it. I was mighty
damn' mad when I heard the will read, it giving the running of
the Rafter D over to Celia until I was twenty-five. Armand
always treated me like I was the worst cowhand he had. If
there was a dirty job on the ranch, I got it, so I figured I might
as well work for somebody else rather than to stay at home.

That's why I lit out for Steamboat Springs."

"It also was the main reason Molly broke her engagement to you and encouraged Dick Lamar," Jean said. "It's like I told you a while ago. Molly didn't aim to live on a cowhand's wages for three years."

Morgan nodded, understanding that Molly would feel that way. He said: "A few weeks ago I got to thinking how the will read and that my birthday was coming up, so I wrote to Lamar. I didn't want any part of the spread, knowing I couldn't work with Armand, but I did want some money. With Lamar being the administrator of the estate, I figured he'd know what Celia would do, so I told him I'd sell my half of the Rafter D for a reasonable figure in cash. I said I was going out to Oregon and have my own spread. That was why he sent for me, saying Celia would buy me out and for me to ride into town quiet-like and stay off Main Street. He said Celia wanted to deal with me and not bring Armand into the dickering, and that, if Armand saw me in town, there would be a hell of a ruckus."

"There would be, too," Jean said. "He's the meanest man in the basin. He's worse than when you knew him."

"I didn't think that was possible," Morgan said. "Well, I didn't have any idea what Celia would offer me, but nobody could call one thousand dollars a reasonable figure. That was what Lamar said Celia would give me. He had the money all counted out and in a canvas bag. Celia was talking about me getting five thousand. I guess Lamar must have stolen four thousand dollars. I got sore and lost my head, or I wouldn't have left town the way I did. I should have gone to Ed Smith as soon as I figured out what Lamar was up to, but I didn't. Likewise, I made a mistake riding out to the Rafter D which was probably what Armand and Celia figured I'd do. I think Armand aimed to kill me."

132

"It would be like him," Jean said.

He rose and rubbed his face. "I'm still not thinking straight. I'll be all right as soon as I get a little sleep."

Jean rose. "Morgan, did you ever kill a woman?"

"No. I'm not going to kill Molly, if that's what you're thinking about."

She nodded. "It was exactly what I was thinking. You've got plenty of reason to break her neck. I'm ashamed of myself, but I hate her. I've hated her ever since I was a child. She'd always been a lying, bitchy girl. She didn't change any when she grew up. What I'm trying to say is that it would get you into trouble if you killed her. She isn't worth it."

Funny thing, he told himself. He felt that he could kill Dick Lamar and Buck Armand, but he guessed that he felt sorry for Molly. Jean was thinking how she felt toward her sister and transferring those feelings to him.

"I won't do anything to her," he said.

Jean nodded, frowning. Molly must have hurt her a great deal, Morgan told himself. When he thought about his sister Celia and the way she had treated him, he could understand how and why Jean felt about Molly the way she did. He had known families in which there had been love and respect and understanding, but it had not been either his or Jean's luck to be born into such a family.

Jean led the way to a bedroom door and opened it. "You can sleep here," she said. "I'll wake you in an hour."

He followed her and sprawled across the bed, the moon throwing a pool of light across its foot. He fell asleep at once. It seemed only a moment later when Jean shook him awake.

"Get up, Morgan," she said. "Somebody's outside. In the barn."

XI

Ed Smith strode to the back door of the Rafter D ranch house, Tully Bean and Johnny Bedlow following. He wondered what he could say to a man like Buck Armand. The trouble was it wasn't just Buck Armand. He would be talking to Celia Dill Armand, to the ghost of old Abe Dill, in the tradition of arrogant power that had been built up over the years.

They crossed the back porch to the door, their spurs jingling. Ed knocked. Celia opened the door and stood there, her body almost filling the opening as she stared at Ed. She made no effort to step aside or to hide her hostility.

"I want to talk to Buck," Ed said.

"He's busy," Celia said in the arrogant way Ed had come to expect of everyone connected with the Rafter D. "What do you want to talk to him about?"

Ed looked past her to Armand, who was seated at the table, his left hand in a basin of water. He looked at Ed coldly, his face a mask of cuts and bruises. Suddenly Ed didn't care whether Celia was a woman or not. She had always acted as if she wanted to be a man and thought of herself as a man, and now he decided to treat her like one. Besides, he was filled up to overflowing with Rafter D's pride and arrogance.

He lowered a shoulder and plowed into her, spinning her out of the doorway and slamming her against the wall. He strode straight across the room to Armand, watching him closely to see if he intended to draw his gun. He didn't look back, sensing that Tully and Johnny Bedlow had moved into the room behind him and would stop Celia from attacking him.

"I see you got tangled with a buzz saw," Ed said.

134

Armand was naked to the waist. A bottle of liniment was on the table next to the basin of water. Ed wished he had seen the fight. Morgan must have been hurt, but he had done a job hurting Buck Armand.

"You can see anything you want to," Armand grunted through swollen lips. "Just say your spiel and git."

"What happened when Morgan came out here?" Ed asked.

"None of your business," Armand snapped. "Turn around and slope out of here. I ain't answering any questions."

"Then put on your shirt," Ed said. "You look pretty well banged up, so we'll saddle a horse for you and head back to town. After you cool your heels for a while in one of our private rooms, you'll be glad to answer any questions I can think of."

"You think you're big enough to take me to jail?" Armand demanded.

"It's not a matter of what I think," Ed said. "We were talking just before we came in, Tully and me, about whether you or my office runs the basin. If you've got some doubts, which in the past you and Celia seem to have had . . . and old Abe had 'em, too . . . then I aim to settle 'em. As far as the law is concerned, my office does all the running. If you try to make your brand of law stick, I'll lock you up in jail so fast it'll make your head swim."

"That's pretty strong liquor you've been drinking," Armand said.

Celia had been standing close to the wall near the door. Now she moved to where Ed stood in front of Armand. "I'll tell you some things you'd better remember," she said. "It ain't a matter of who runs the basin. There's some things we won't allow and you'd better understand that now. We both know there was something wrong with Pa's will that left half of the Rafter D to Morgan. I ain't sure what it was. Or let's say I can't prove what it was, but I've got a hunch Judge Alcorn could tell you. Anyhow, we ain't giving any part of the outfit to Morgan. I was the one who took care of Pa. Me 'n' Buck here kept the spread going while all Morgan done was to horse around and raise hell. He deserves nothing and that's what he's gonna get."

"I didn't ride out here to argue with you about the will and Morgan," Ed said. "The court will take care of that. I'm looking for Morgan and I want to know what happened when he showed up and where he went after he left."

"He had a fight with Buck," Celia said. "I fetched Buck into the house and wiped off some of the blood. He sprained his left hand on Morgan's head and he's soaking it in hot water. Morgan rode off. We don't know where he went."

"What did Morgan do that put you on his tail?" Armand asked. "Did he rob the bank or something like that?"

Ed wondered why he would ask that question. He studied Armand's battered face for a moment, then he said: "We want him for questioning. I talked to Slim Turner before he left. He said you were sending him to Indian Springs to get the crew. Why?"

"We're gonna hunt Morgan," Armand said. "When we find him, we'll hang him. If he's hiding out in some house in town, we'll burn the town if it takes that to run him out of his hole. He stole the buckskin gelding he's riding when he left the basin three years ago. It's a Rafter D horse. You always hang a man for horse stealing, don't you?"

The horse had belonged to Morgan from the time it had been a colt. The sheer effrontery of Armand's words shocked Ed, even though he had been familiar with the Rafter D's attitude toward law enforcement for a long time. He said: "Buck, this is what I've been trying to tell you. You lay a hand on Morgan . . . I don't care what the charge is . . . and I'll put you in jail. Not one of your crew. You! If you do hang Morgan, you'll be tried for murder."

"That's big talk, Sheriff," Armand said easily. "You were singing pretty low for a long time. How come you're talking so big now?"

Ed wasn't sure. He had swallowed his pride just as Judge Alcorn had, but after about so long a man discovers he can't go on swallowing. He has to do something. He had reached that point.

"Let's just say it's taken me a long time to get around to talking big," Ed answered. "If you figure I can't do it, stand up and make your play. Your right hand's in good shape."

Armand shook his head. "And take on three men? I ain't that good. Or that stupid. No, I'll wait till my boys get here and we'll see who's talking big. If you're trying to scare us into giving Morgan half of the Rafter D, it won't work, Sheriff."

"One thing, and you'd better think about it," Ed said. "You couldn't handle Morgan by yourself. You fetch your whole crew in to take one man and you and the Rafter D will be the laughingstock of the basin."

Ed wheeled and strode out of the house. He didn't say a word as he mounted and rode away, but he was sour-tempered, knowing he hadn't really accomplished anything. As far as cutting the Rafter D down to size, he hadn't even started. It was a job that would take some powder burning.

In the past he had let the situation drift. It had gone too far because it had been the easy thing to do. Now he thought about his wife and children; he thought about Morgan Dill and the unfairness of this situation in which he had been forced to look for a desperate man who might be innocent.

Well, if he was going to get killed, he'd rather do it making his stand for the principle of law enforcement against the Rafter D than trying to arrest Morgan Dill.

When he reached the road, he reined up. He said: "Tully, looks to me like we'll be swapping lead with the whole Rafter D pack of wolves before sunup. I wish we had Morgan's gun on our side."

"So do I," Tully said. "I sure do."

"Morgan's going to get his half of the outfit," Ed said. "He'll make that will stand up in court. Well, you figure Morgan's still down here in the willows?"

If he were, he would hear what they were saying. Somehow it seemed of utmost importance for Morgan to hear, for him to know that they were his allies against Buck Armand and the Rafter D crew. But Tully, who had been examining the road, turned and said: "He went back to town. Leastwise somebody did recent-like. It must have been Morgan."

Ed nodded wearily. He guessed he had expected it. Now they faced the task of hunting Morgan in town where there were a dozen places for him to hide. The chances were Armand and his men would be hunting him before sunup, too.

"We'll get along to town and start looking," Ed said, "but I don't know where to start."

"Maybe with Lamar," Tully said. "Morg will make him talk or kill him."

"And then he'll face a murder charge," Ed said. "We'd better find him first."

"It sure done me good to hear you talking back there," Tully said. "I never was able to figure out why you and Judge Alcorn and everybody else kept pussyfooting around with that Rafter D outfit."

Ed didn't answer. He really didn't have an answer. Maybe

it had become a habit. Or maybe Ed and Alcorn and the rest wanted to live so much they had been afraid to face the situation. All Ed knew for sure was that he was off his knees at last and he felt like a man for the first time in years. It was a good feeling, a hell of a good feeling. He wondered if Judge Alcorn and Sam Colter and the rest of the Twin Rocks people would ever have that feeling.

XII

Ed rode back to town in silence, Tully and Johnny Bedlow trailing him. It was going to be a long night, he thought, if they didn't get lucky and find Morgan. He judged they had until about dawn before Buck Armand would lead his men into Twin Rocks. Suppose that he hadn't found Morgan by that time? What would Armand do?

He turned this over in his mind as he rode. He got sick after he had thought about it a while. Armand was crazy, crazy enough to be convinced that he was above the law and could do anything and not be held responsible for it. Knowing that, Ed came to the only conclusion he could. Armand would burn the town, just as he had threatened, if he couldn't find Morgan.

How did you stop a man like Armand? Even if Ed persuaded Morgan to throw in with them, there were only four men to do the fighting. He knew and Armand knew that the town fathers like Judge Alcorn and Sam Colter and Baldy Miles would run for cover. They'd be worth nothing when it came to the final showdown. Well, there was only one thing he could do. Find Morgan and jail him for his own safety, then put a gun in his hand when it was time for the shooting to start. That was the only way he might prevent disaster, and he wasn't sure that would do the job. The odds were just too long.

When they reached the edge of town, Ed said: "We'll start at Dick Lamar's house. I don't think we'll find Morgan there, but it's like you said, Tully. It's the logical place where he'd start. If we're too late and he's killed Lamar, then there'll be hell to pay all around."

Lamar's house was on a side street one block from the bank. It was the biggest and finest residence in Twin Rocks, which was fitting for the town banker and had been one of the reasons that Molly Runyan had married Lamar. She had given some great parties here, or so Ed had heard. He didn't know from personal experience because he and his wife didn't belong to the select social set that was invited to Molly's parties, and that suited him and his wife perfectly.

The three men tied up at the hitch pole in front, Ed's gaze on the house that in the moonlight was a sort of ghostly monument to Lamar's position in the town's pecking order. It was a two-story structure with a mansard roof, the only brick residence in town. An iron fence ran along the front of the lawn. Ed glanced up at the balcony with its white balustrade and shook his head, wondering if Molly ever regretted not marrying Morgan and if she was happy, now that she had gone as high as she could in Twin Rocks' society. She probably wasn't happy at all, Ed guessed, and more than likely had nagged Lamar about moving to Denver where she would have a new world to conquer. She'd never get there, Ed thought, if the gossip about the condition of Lamar's bank was true.

They crossed the porch. Ed yanked the bell pull, and, when no one answered, he yanked three more times. The glass in the front door was frosted, so he didn't have a clear view into the back of the house, but there was a light back there somewhere. Now it seemed to be moving forward along the hall. A moment later the door opened and Lamar stood there, a lamp in his hand, and peered at the men who stood in front of him as if uncertain about what he would say and do.

"We want to talk to you," Ed said.

"I sure as hell don't want to talk to you," Lamar snarled. "All I give a damn about as far as the sheriff's office is concerned is getting Morgan Dill locked up in a cell."

"That's why we're here," Ed said. "Can we come in?"

"No," Lamar snapped. "I'm getting ready for bed. Molly has a headache. So have I, after what happened today. I don't know what I'm going to do. I don't have enough money to even open the bank in the morning."

Lamar started to shut the door, but Ed shoved his foot against it. He said: "We're coming in, Lamar. You'll have a bigger headache if you don't talk to us."

"Have you got a warrant?" Lamar screeched. "A man's home is his castle. You've got no right to force your way in here if you. . . ."

Ed's patience snapped. Lamar had always irritated him. Now the irritation turned into fury. He smashed a shoulder against the nearly closed door, slamming it open and sending Lamar reeling back so that he almost dropped the lamp.

"Come on," Ed said to Tully and Johnny Bedlow. "Lamar just invited us in."

He strode along the hall to the back of the house where an open door showed a light. He had never been inside the house before, but he guessed there was some sort of study or sitting room in the back. He was right. Molly was sitting on a rosewood sofa, some embroidery on her lap.

He judged that it was Molly's private sitting room with its rocking chairs, their seats covered by thick cushions, the wine-red carpet, and the sewing machine that, he guessed, she seldom used. The paintings on the wall were of brightly colored flowers, each surrounded by a heavy gilt frame. A melodeon was set against the far wall, and he remembered that Molly had always been fond of music.

"Good evening, Sheriff," Molly said. "I hear Morgan is back in town."

"That's right," Ed said. "How's your headache?"

She was surprised. "Why, I don't have a headache right now. Why did you ask?"

"Your husband said you did."

She laughed. "Well, Dick lies a lot."

Lamar came in just as she said that and set the lamp on a claw-footed walnut stand in the middle of the room. "Sure I lied," he said. "I didn't want you in here upsetting our evening. Smith, you've made yourself a hell of a lot of trouble. I'm going to take this up with Judge Alcorn in the morning. I'll have you thrown out of office for breaking into my house. I don't have to stand for this, and I won't."

Ed nodded at Tully who was standing in the doorway, Johnny a step behind him. He said: "Tully, you and Johnny take this lamp and search the house to make sure that Morgan isn't in it somewhere. Look in places where Lamar could hide a body."

"My God!" Molly screamed. "You think we'd kill Morgan? I haven't even seen him. Anyhow, he's the last man in the world I'd want killed."

"I doubt that your husband feels the same way," Ed said dryly.

Lamar was speechless for a moment, his eyes bugging from his head. Then he said in a choked voice: "This is the damnedest outrage I was ever subjected to. Just who do you think you are, Smith?"

"I guess I could ask you the same question," Ed said, "but right now all I want is to know where Morgan is."

"You're looking in a mighty funny place," Lamar snapped. "Why do you think you'd find him here?"

"Because he's going to come here sooner or later to make you clear him of the bank robbery charge," Ed answered. "If it got to the place where you had a fight, he'd kill you or you'd kill him. I can see you're alive, so I figure there's a chance you got him and you hid the body until you could decide what to do with it later on."

Lamar snorted a laugh. "I never heard such hogwash in my life. He robbed me and lit out with the money. One thing you can count on is that he's too smart to stay around here."

"Your story don't hold up, Lamar," Ed said. "It's like Molly said a while ago. You lie a lot."

The banker wheeled to face his wife. "Why in God's name did you say that?"

For a moment Molly didn't answer. She continued embroidering, her eyes on the circle of cloth tightened between the two hoops. She was a beautiful woman, Ed thought. She was wearing a belted blue wrapper; her hair hung down her back in a shining black mass; her features were perfect by Ed's standards. Yet for all of her beauty, he sensed that she was far from contented. He had heard stories of her verbal battles with her husband. The neighbors told of hearing them screaming at each other far into the night.

Finally she looked up at Lamar. "Because you do lie a lot. I know that you've never told me the truth about what you do in Grand Junction when you go there. I know that you've gambled and lost more money than you've ever admitted to anyone, and I believe you've slept with whores every time you've been in Grand Junction and lied to me when you came home."

"It's not true!" Lamar shouted. "It's not true at all. I told the truth about Morgan Dill holding me up. Now I'm broke, I tell you! The bank won't be able to open in the morning."

Ed shook his head. "It won't work, Lamar. Morg would be a fool to stop and hold up a bank when he came back at the time he was to inherit half of the Rafter D. Being a fool is one thing Morg isn't."

Lamar snorted. "You know Celia. She made him a piddling offer for his half of the ranch. He could take it or leave it. If he didn't take it, he got nothing. You know damned well that Armand wouldn't let him on the place. Dill knew it, too. Well, he aimed to get more than the five thousand dollars Celia offered him, so he took it the only way he could, by poking a gun into my belly."

"And I know Morgan," Molly said. "I don't believe he's capable of robbing a bank, yours or anyone else's."

"Maybe you knew him once," Lamar said, "but you don't know him now. He's a bad one, I tell you. He'd have killed me this evening without batting an eye. I was never so scared in my life. Now he's ten miles from here, Smith, and you're not even trying to find him. In the morning I aim to let this town know how you enforce the law."

Tully and Johnny Bedlow came into the room, Tully setting the lamp down. He said: "We didn't find nothing, Ed. I don't think he's here."

For a moment Ed stood looking down at Molly, wondering what Lamar would do to her after he left. He said: "Will you be all right, Molly?"

She looked up at him, surprised, her full red lips slightly parted. "Of course."

"Then I guess we'll look somewhere else," Ed said.

He wheeled and left the room, Tully and Johnny Bedlow following.

XIII

For a time Ed stood beside his horse, one hand on the horn as he tried to bring back into his mind everything that he could remember about Morgan Dill. It would take all night to search the barns in Twin Rocks. Almost every house had one. He didn't have all night, so the problem was where to start.

At last Ed said: "I never knew Morg as well as you two did. I've been trying to think where he'd go after being gone so long. He never had many friends in town except you boys. Now he's in trouble. He's probably hurting in a dozen places after his fight with Armand. He needs help, maybe something to eat and a drink, maybe some liniment and bandages. Now where would he go to get help?"

"I've been asking myself the same thing," Tully said. "I don't know, Ed. I just don't know. He won't go to Doc Bridges. He hated the old buzzard. He might go to my place. Or Johnny's."

"Not to mine," Johnny said quickly. "I was an idiot tonight, not shaking hands with him, but it's too late now. He probably thinks I don't want nothing to do with him."

"Well, mine then," Tully said. "He may figure that, even if I am a deputy, I wouldn't turn him in."

"All right," Ed said. "You go have a look at your place, Tully. Johnny and me will try the stables. I don't think he'd leave his horse in one of the stables, but we've got to make sure."

"If he's hurting bad," Johnny said, "he might leave his horse in a stable and crawl up into the mow, or maybe take a hotel room."

"No, he wouldn't do that," Tully said sharply. "If I know

Morg, he'd have to just about be dead to do anything of the kind."

"We'll find out," Ed said. "I'll have a look at the Red Front stable. Johnny, you try Barney's. We'll wait for each other in front of the courthouse."

A few minutes later Ed rode through the archway of the Red Front stable and dismounted. A lantern was hanging from the wall just inside the door. He took it down and walked slowly along the runway, examining each horse, but he recognized most of them. None of the ones he didn't know was a buckskin gelding.

He went on out through the back door and checked the corral, but he still failed to find a horse that could have been Morgan's. There were several bays, a couple of blacks, and one sorrel, but no buckskins. This was what he expected, but still he was disappointed.

As Ed strode back along the runway, Uncle Joe Miller, the owner of the stable, came out of the little room that served as an office and held a cot that he slept on when he stayed in the stable overnight. He rubbed his eyes and squinted at Ed.

"I heered somebody prowling around out here," Miller said in his squeaky voice. "Now just what the hell are you up to this time of night? I reckon you ain't here to trade horses, are you?"

"No, I sure ain't," Ed agreed. "I'm looking for Morgan Dill. I thought maybe he'd left his horse here and got a hotel room."

"Dill?" Miller said. "I didn't know that young hellion was back in town. If he is, he can leave his horse somewhere else. I remember the time he set a bucket of water over the door of my office and tied a string to the doorknob. I came in late one night to go to bed, so tired I could hardly move, and damned if I didn't get soaked to the skin. What he couldn't think of, that damned depity of your'n could. Or Johnny Bedlow. No, sir, I ain't seen young Dill, and I ain't hankerin' to.'"

"All right, Joe," Ed said. "Go back to bed."

He mounted and rode the half block to the hotel, dismounted, and went inside. No one was behind the desk, so he tapped the bell, then gave the register a turn and checked the names of everyone who had registered that day. Morgan Dill was not among them, but that, of course, proved nothing.

A big woman came out of a room back of the lobby, stretching and yawning and scratching herself, then she saw who was at the desk and stopped, her face flushed with anger. "Well, by God, if it ain't the law. Now don't tell me your pretty wife kicked you out of your bed because you've been horsing around and you're looking for one?"

"Amanda," Ed said, "you can take a good mood in a man and turn it into a sour one without even trying. What you need is competition."

She laughed. "Naw, competition wouldn't change me for the better. Might even make me worse. Besides, no sense in two of us starving to death when I can do it by myself. It's enough for me to wonder how I'm gonna keep Dick Lamar and his stinking bank from taking over the hotel."

"I'm looking for Morgan Dill," Ed said. "I thought he might have taken a room here."

"Morgan?" She shook her head. "I didn't know he was back in town. I sure ain't seen hide nor hair of him. Say, did he come back to settle with that son-of-a-bitch of a sister of his?"

"He's back," Ed said, "and Lamar claims he robbed the bank. I've got to find him and talk to him before Buck Armand does."

"Can't help you," the woman said. "I wish I could. Morgan used to make some of the old fuddy-duddies mad the

148

way he tore around, but I always liked his style. On the other hand, I wouldn't believe anything Dick Lamar said if he was standing on a knee-high stack of Bibles."

"Sorry I had to wake you up," Ed said.

"You're a liar," she said amiably. "You enjoyed doing it."

Ed grinned. "All right. I enjoyed it."

He walked out of the lobby, stepped up, and rode to the courthouse. Tully and Johnny were waiting for him.

"Any luck?" Ed asked.

"Not any," Tully said.

Johnny nodded. "Same here."

"Well, I guess I didn't expect any," Ed said sourly. "I just hoped we'd have some. Nothing to do but look in every barn in town and we just don't have that much time. Morgan wouldn't leave his horse outside for one of us to find." He paused and scratched the back of his neck thoughtfully. "Maybe we can figure out which barns he wouldn't use."

"He wouldn't use Judge Alcorn's," Tully said, "or Doc Bridges's. Outside of them two, I don't know which one he'd pick or wouldn't pick. He might take one at random."

"At first I didn't think he'd go to Lamar's place," Ed said, "but now I figure he will. He was always short on patience. I can't see him wasting the night."

"Wait a minute," Johnny said. "I've got an idea. You recollect who you talked to this evening? I mean . . . in front of the bank?"

Ed stared at him blankly for a moment, then he remembered Jean Runyan's stopping him as he'd left the bank. "Yeah, I saw Jean Runyan, but what's that got to do with Morgan?"

"She knew he was in town," Johnny said. "She was almighty worried about him, so she must have been friendly with him. Morg would know that, so he might go to her place."

"Hell, yes," Ed said. "I should have thought of that sooner. We'll try it."

They rode to the end of the block, then turned off Main Street and rode up an alley past the rear of dark houses until they reached the Runyan barn. A light was burning in the kitchen, so Jean was still up. Ed wondered about that as he swung down.

"Johnny, stay with the horses," Ed ordered. "Tully, me and you will ease around the corner into the barn. I don't want Jean to let go at us with a shotgun."

Ed slipped around the corner of the barn, pausing a moment as he studied the lighted kitchen window and the fifty feet or more of back yard that was brightly lighted by the moon. No one could reach the rear of the house without being seen. If Morgan was inside and he saw anyone approaching the house, he'd cut loose with his six-shooter. At this distance and with this light, he couldn't miss.

Very slowly and gently Ed gave the turn pin a twist and opened the door, hearing the squeal of rusty hinges that seemed inordinately loud to his ears. He slipped inside, waited for Tully to follow, then closed and hooked the door shut. He scratched a match to life, jacked up the chimney of a lantern that hung near the door, and lighted the wick. He eased the chimney down, then heard Tully swear softly.

"That's his horse, all right," Tully said. "I'd know that gelding anywhere. I've rode beside him too many times to be mistook."

"Then he's inside," Ed said. "I'd gamble on it. That was a good hunch Johnny had."

He moved along the wall to where Morgan had left his saddle. For a moment he stood staring at the saddlebags, afraid of what he'd find in them. He took a long breath, opened them, and took out a canvas sack marked Twin Rocks

Bank. He groaned, and said in a low tone: "Well, this is the last thing I wanted to find."

Tully whistled. "Well, now, you don't think Lamar told the truth for once in his life?"

"Looks like it," Ed said.

He opened the sack and drew out a handful of gold coins. "I dunno, Tully," he said heavily, "I sure don't. I'll want to talk to Morgan before I make up my mind about him, but this looks bad. It's the kind of evidence that would make a jury send him to the Canon City pen."

Tully shook his head. "I still don't believe it, Ed. I just don't think a man like Morgan can change that much."

Ed wondered how much money was in the sack, and decided it couldn't be more than $800 or $900, $1,000 at the most. He said, "If we take this sack to Lamar and tell him where we found it, he'd say it proved his story and proves that Morgan's guilty, so we won't do no such thing. It strikes me that Lamar must have had more than this in the bank, and, if Morgan had cleaned his safe out the way he said, Morgan would have more."

"That's right," Tully said. "Let's go talk to him."

"Not just yet," Ed said. "Not unless you want to be the first to go to the back door."

Tully grinned. "No, I can't say I do. Old Morg might be in the kitchen, watching with his iron in hand."

"Then we'll wait a spell," Ed said, "till we figure out how to get there without getting plugged."

XIV

For a time Morgan could not comprehend what Jean was telling him. He felt as if he were fighting his way upward through a suffocating blanket of fog. Jean shook him again, and her words beat against his ears: "Morgan, you've got to wake up. Somebody's in the barn. I don't know who it is, but it might be Buck Armand and some of his crew."

He sat up, and shook his head. His body ached in a dozen places where Armand's big fists had slugged him. Jean had not brought a lamp with her, but light fell through the open door from the kitchen. The pool of moonlight, too, was still on the foot of the bed. Still, she was an indistinct shape to him. He rubbed his eyes and blinked, but he could not bring her into sharp focus.

"Wait a minute," he said. "My head's fogged up. I just now got to sleep."

"You've been asleep for more than an hour," she said sharply. "I was sitting on the back porch when I heard horses in the alley. The men dismounted. They were talking, but they kept their voices so low I couldn't make out what they were saying. Two of them went into the barn and closed the door."

His head was gradually clearing and everything that had happened since his arrival in Twin Rocks came back to him. His buckskin gelding was in the barn. Buck Armand or the sheriff or almost anyone would recognize the horse and would guess that he was around here somewhere.

He stood up. "I don't want to go out there and start shooting unless I have to. You might get hurt. If it's Armand, I'll have to. If it's the sheriff or someone else, maybe I won't. You go to the back porch and ask who it is. Let them come

152

into the house if they want to. I'll stay here and keep the door open a crack so I can see what's going on. If they come in and start roughing you up to make you tell them where I am, I'll take a hand in the game."

She hesitated, her worried gaze on him. Suddenly her hands went out to him and gripped his shoulders. She said: "Morgan, if it's the sheriff, I want you to talk to him. I know Ed Smith. So do you. He's an honest man. You can't go on running from him and Buck Armand."

"Sure, he's an honest man," Morgan said bitterly, "but men like Dick Lamar and Judge Alcorn and the rest of the big roosters in town call the turn, and Ed listens. No, the only chance I've got is to make Lamar clear me. Don't tell them I'm here under any circumstances. It will make me burn some powder if you do and I don't want that."

Still she hesitated as if she knew he was wrong, but she didn't press it. She shook her head, saying—"I don't know why the good Lord ever created stubborn men."—and left the bedroom.

He closed the door, then moved across the room to the back window that looked out upon the yard. He heard Jean call: "Who's out there?"

Silence for a good minute, then a man answered. "It's Ed Smith, Jean. Tully's with me. We want to talk to you."

"Come on in," she said. "You can talk to me any time, even at one o'clock in the morning."

Silence again for a moment. Morgan guessed that Smith and Tully were talking it over. They probably were convinced he was in the house and were afraid he would start shooting the moment he saw them. Finally Smith yelled: "Jean, is Morgan with you?"

"No, of course not," she answered. "What makes you think he's here?"

"His horse is in the barn."

"He is?" she said as if surprised. "Well, maybe he's asleep out there somewhere."

Both men stepped out of the barn and ran toward the back porch, more afraid than ever, Morgan thought, that he'd open up on them any minute. Still, they had taken the chance, so they were gambling on his not shooting them. He quickly moved back to the door and opened it a crack, then drew his gun.

Jean was in the kitchen, standing by the stove. She asked as Smith came in: "Will you have a cup of coffee, Sheriff?"

"Sure will," Smith said, his gaze whipping around the room, fixing on the bedroom door for a moment, then going back to Jean. "You're sure Morgan ain't here?"

"Sure I'm sure," she said testily. "I ought to know who's in my house. Besides, he left town."

Tully came in then and remained near the back door. Neither man had changed, Morgan thought. He had never been particularly fond of Smith, but he had been very close to Tully and he found it hard to believe that his old friend had actually taken the deputy's job.

He wondered where Johnny Bedlow was. Probably in the alley somewhere, he decided, or maybe he'd gone around to the front to cut him off if he made a run for it. He doubted that Smith believed Jean, but that wasn't important. What was important was whether the sheriff would insist on searching the house. It meant trouble if he did, and right now Morgan wanted to avoid trouble with everybody except Dick Lamar.

Jean poured two cups of coffee and handed them to Smith and Tully, then she asked: "Just what were you two pussy-footing around in my barn for? I don't think I like that. If you've got something on your mind, you could come to the door and ask like men."

"We were looking for Morgan's horse, figuring that he'd be where his horse was," Smith said. "We know he went to the Rafter D and we thought he came back to town. Now that we've found his horse, we know he did."

Jean shrugged. "Like I said, I thought he'd left town, but I guess he is around here somewhere if his horse is in my barn."

Smith walked to the table and sat down. He said: "We've got to find him, Jean. Armand has sent for his crew and he'll bring 'em into town and tear the place apart till he finds Morgan."

"What will he do then?" Jean demanded.

"He says he'll hang Morgan for horse stealing," Smith said. "He claims that Morgan stole the buckskin, that the animal belongs to the Rafter D."

"That's ridiculous!" Jean cried. "Why, Morgan's had that horse for a long time. I remember him riding the horse when he was shining up to Molly."

"I know, I know," Smith said impatiently. "The trouble is, Armand's gone loco. He's got his greedy hands on the Rafter D and he don't aim to let go. He's worse now that Morgan gave him a whipping."

"He's got to let go of half of it," Jean said. "That half belongs to Morgan."

"That's the point," Smith said. "He won't settle for Celia's half. If Morgan stays alive, he can take his share, so Armand's bound to find an excuse to kill him. Horse stealing will do."

"You'd have to bring him in for murder," Jean said. "He ought to know he can't get away with anything as wild as that."

"Armand is going to be hard to bring in on any charge," Smith said. "I've got one deputy. I can call on Johnny Bedlow and that's about the size of it. Everybody is scared of Buck Armand and you know it as well as I do. The Rafter D bull-dozed this county for years when old Abe was alive. Well, Armand's worse because he's crazy and Abe wasn't."

"Are you sitting there telling me that Armand can ride in here with his crew and hang Morgan on a trumped-up charge like that and get away scotfree?" Jean shook her head. "Ed, you wouldn't let him?"

"How can three men stop him?" Smith demanded sourly.

She stood there, shaking her head. Tully said: "Jean, Morg was my best friend. I don't aim for Armand to get his hands on him, but you've got to help. We can protect Morgan if we can find him. If Armand finds him first, we can't. We want Morgan to give himself up."

"And just what will you do with him if he does?" Jean demanded.

"We'll put him in jail for his own protection," Tully said. "If Armand tries to break him out, we'll give Morgan a gun because he'll need it."

"If Armand finds out we don't have Morgan in jail," Smith said, "he'll burn the town, figuring that will make him show himself. If Morgan is in jail, the four of us can hold Armand off. I think we can whip him."

Morgan saw Jean wipe her eyes and for a terrible moment he thought she was going to give him away. One thing was certain. He wasn't going to jail. They might be on the level. He had never known Tully to lie to him. Still, he wasn't sure that Ed Smith saw the situation the way Tully did.

Tully and Smith were watching Jean. She was silent, biting her lower lip and dabbing at her eyes. Then Tully said: "Jean, you're bound to see Morgan since his horse is here. You know, and Morgan would know if he was here to hear me say it, that there's nothing I wouldn't do for him. Right now he's got a chance to do something for himself and the town. We need him. Now you tell him that."

"He didn't rob the bank!" Jean cried. "I'll never believe that he did. He'll find some way to make Lamar clear him. It seems to me that you'd do a better job if you got the truth out of Dick Lamar."

"We will," Smith promised. "We don't think Morgan robbed the bank, either, but right now Buck Armand is the dangerous man, not Lamar."

Jean threw up her hands. "All right, do it your way. I'll tell Morgan if I see him. Now why don't you go on back to the courthouse or go home or wherever you want to. I'm ready for bed."

Smith rose. "We'll go back to the courthouse. Get word to Morgan that we're expecting him." He started toward the door, then stopped. "Seems funny that you're up so late."

"Nothing funny about it," she snapped. "I couldn't sleep for worrying about Morgan and I'm still worrying. What you've told me about Armand doesn't help. I still probably won't be able to sleep."

"Just get word to Morgan that we need him," Smith said. "With his help, we can clean Armand's plow for him." He left.

Tully followed, until he reached the door, then he turned. "I'm not sure you believe us, Jean, but you've got to. What's more, you've got to convince Morgan that we're still his friends."

He went out. Jean didn't move until they were out of the light, then she left the house and crossed the yard to the barn. She returned in a few minutes and shut the kitchen door. She said: "They're gone, Morgan. You can come out now."

XV

After Ed Smith and his men left the house, Lamar returned to Molly's sitting room and stood looking down at her. To him she was the most beautiful and desirable woman in the world. He still loved her; at least he loved her as much as he was capable of loving any woman. The first year of their marriage had been wonderful, the happiest year of his life, but then something happened.

He was not sure what had gone wrong. Molly had been a lusty wanton in bed, then for no reason that he could put his finger on she had turned cold. That was the reason, he had told himself, that he had started going to Grand Junction, the reason for his gambling, the reason for his bedding down with cheap whores. There were lines of discontent around her eyes that had not been there when they were married. Her mouth used to turn up at the corners in a ready smile when he came home from the bank. Now it curled down in derision. She had not given a party for three months, and, when he pressed her for the reason, she had said languidly that she was too tired.

Suddenly all the bitterness and frustration that had been piling up in him boiled over. He said: "Why in God's name did you tell Smith I lied a lot? Were you trying to make him think I was lying about Dill holding me up?"

She had been working steadily on her embroidery, ignoring him as completely as if he wasn't in the room. Now she glanced up. "Why, yes, darling. That's exactly what I wanted him to think. You were lying, weren't you? You framed Morgan, didn't you?"

"Sure I did, but they don't know it," he said. "I can make it stick, too. I can send Dill to the pen for twenty years, and I can get Alcorn and Colter and some of the others to back me in starting a new bank. Do you hear, Molly? We can start over."

"No." She went on with her embroidery. "We can't start over. We're finished. You're finished in this town, too, and I can't stand a failure. I can't stand living in this stinking, dirty, little town, either."

This, he knew, was part of the trouble, although he had never taken it seriously. Now, looking at her flushed face, he knew that it had been a mistake. Maybe that was what had turned their marriage sour. She had been contented and happy that first year, then she seemed to feel she had done all she could in Twin Rocks and began nagging him about selling the bank and moving to Denver. He had never seriously considered it and had told her to shut up about it. They were living in Twin Rocks and she'd better be happy to have the best house in town.

He clenched his fists and wheeled around and walked across the room and back. He knew she was right about being finished in Twin Rocks. There had been too much talk about his trips to Grand Junction, too many rumors about the bank being on thin ice. Some of it had come back to him; there must be a great deal of it going around the community.

He hunkered down in front of her and took her hands. He said: "Listen to me, Molly. I love you. I don't want to give you up. We'll leave here. You've been wanting to go away. Now we'll do it."

She left her hands in his, limp and without life. Her eyes were scornful as she said: "What will we use for money? You're broke, aren't you?"

"Not quite," he answered. "I've got a paper that Buck Armand and Celia want. Dill signed it when he was in the bank this evening. It says that he gives up his share to the

Rafter D for the money I gave him. It's worth five thousand dollars to Armand. I know they've got that much cash out there. Five thousand will take us a long ways."

"And what will we do then?" she demanded.

"I'll make more," he promised. "I've got ways of making money. I guess I'm as tired of Twin Rocks as you are. If we go somewhere else, some place where I'm not known, I can do all right. You know that. I did all right until you drove me away."

"Me drive you away?" She jerked her hands away from his. "Why are you blaming me? I didn't drive you anywhere."

"The hell you didn't."

He rose and backed away from her, hating her and wanting to put his hands on her white throat and choke the life out of her. She must be lying. She was smart. She had to know what she had done to him.

"You know what you've been," he said. "When we were first married, I couldn't have asked for a better wife, then you turned into an iceberg. I might as well have been sleeping with a dead woman."

"That wasn't what drove you away," she said scornfully. "You got big ideas about what you could do playing poker and all you did was lose the bank and your self-respect. Why you'd think I'd even want you to sleep with me is more than I know when I knew what you were doing in Grand Junction."

"You didn't know," he flung at her. "I never told you."

"You didn't have to," she snapped. "I knew, all right. You're crazy if you think that going to some damned whorehouse in Grand Junction would make me welcome you back into my bed."

"It wasn't that in the beginning!" he shouted. "You damned broke me the first year we were married. You spent money like water every time you were in Denver. You've got dresses in your closet you've never worn. Nothing satisfied you, by God, *nothing!*"

Her right hand moved away from her drawing the thread tight, then the needle pierced the cloth, and she drew the thread tight again. Slowly she raised her head and looked at him, smiling in her tantalizing way.

"A banker should be able to support his wife, shouldn't he, darling?" she said.

This was the way she often treated him when they were fighting and it always drove him into a fury. But now he didn't want their conversation to go this way. His fists closed and opened; he felt his heart pounding. He knew he had lost her; still, he could not give up.

"Listen, Molly," he said earnestly, "I'll admit I've done some bad things to you, but I'll change. I promise. I want you to go with me when I leave. I'm going to saddle up and ride out to the Rafter D. I'll get my money and I'll be back before sunup. Will you be ready to go?"

She had started working on her embroidery again. Now she glanced up and nodded. "I'll be ready. What have I got to stay here for?"

"Good. We can start over. You'll see."

He stooped and kissed her. She did not respond. His lips were eager, but she gave nothing back to him. He straightened and again felt the compelling impulse to choke her, or slap her face until her head wobbled. Not now, he told himself. Later, maybe, if she didn't keep her promise.

He left the room and went into his bedroom. He had put away his gun when he'd come home from the bank. Now he opened a bureau drawer and took out the gun and belt. He checked the revolver, saw that there were five loads in the cylinder, and slipped it back into the holster. He looked at it for a time, wondering if he should take it.

He seldom wore a gun, and he wasn't very good with it, but he didn't think Buck Armand was, either. He didn't trust Celia and he trusted Armand even less. He'd better take it, he decided. They might try to cheat him out of his $5,000 and he wasn't standing still for that. He'd earned his money. He would be keeping his part of the agreement by delivering the paper signed by Morgan Dill.

Lamar buckled the gun belt around his waist and left the house, not taking the time to look in on Molly. He strode across the moon-drenched back yard to the barn, lighted a lantern, and saddled his black gelding. He blew out the lantern, led the horse out of the barn, closed the door, and stepped into the saddle.

He did not have any faith in Molly's promise to leave with him, and for the first time he considered going without her. He might just as well keep on riding after he left the Rafter D. He had nothing left here except his personal possessions and the furniture, and he couldn't sell any of it for any worthwhile sum.

The furniture was expensive. He'd bought it new when they were married, but who would buy it for anything like what he had paid? The house was mortgaged for more than it was worth. He wanted to laugh when he thought about it. Molly didn't know about the mortgage. She probably figured she could go right on living there. Well, she was in for a surprise!

He could decide about going on without her after he left the Rafter D. He had to go back through town anyway. Suddenly he was in a hurry. He wanted to get this settled and be on his way. He could no longer face his failure here. It was hard to believe he had actually reached this point.

When they were married, he had the world by the tail and a downhill pull; he was the most powerful and respected man in town. Now he was nothing. Even the stupid sheriff didn't believe his story. No one loved him. By God, when he thought about it, no one even liked him. He didn't have a friend in town. He could lay it all on Molly. Why had he sucked around after her all that time, trying to outmaneuver Morgan Dill and break his engagement to Molly, was more than he could understand.

He put his horse to a gallop, feeling the cool night breeze on his hot face. Why he had even tried to talk Molly into going away with him was more than he knew. He was better off without her. Then, slowly, he began to think about Molly and the first months of their marriage. Her face haunted him. He would never be free of her as long as he lived. No, he had to take her with him. If at the last minute she refused to go, he'd put his hands on her beautiful throat and he'd squeeze until she couldn't breathe. If he couldn't have her, no one else would, either. How could a man both hate and love a woman the way he hated and loved Molly? He didn't know. It made no sense at all, but that was the way it was.

He reached the fork in the road and turned off toward the Rafter D. He had to get his business done and hurry back to Twin Rocks. He had to know what Molly would do.

XVI

Morgan left the bedroom as soon as Jean told him that the sheriff and Tully had gone. Jean asked: "You heard them, didn't you, Morgan?"

"Sure I heard them," he answered. "You didn't believe them, did you?"

"Yes, I did," she said sharply, "and you ought to believe them just as much as I do. I've known both men as long as I can remember, and I know that, if there are two decent men in this world you can believe, it's Ed Smith and Tully Bean."

"There was a time when I would have agreed," Morgan said, "but I figure things are different now. It would be quite a feather in Smith's cap if he could throw me into the jug, and I'd say Tully has sold out to him. Johnny Bedlow, too, I guess."

"No, Morgan." She walked to him and put her hands on his arms. "Now you listen. Ed doesn't need any feathers in his cap, and Tully was and is your best friend. You can't go fighting all of them. You heard what the sheriff said about Buck Armand bringing his men in and that they needed your gun. Help them, Morgan. You'll be helping yourself, too."

He shook his head. "Maybe you're right about Smith not needing any feathers in his cap, but he wants to stay alive, doesn't he? He knows that, if he tries to take me, some of them will be dead. I've got to play it my way, Jean, and stay out of jail. Lamar has framed me and he can make it stick if I don't make him clear me."

"Just how do you think you're going to do that?" she cried. "Morgan, I tried to tell you the kind of man Lamar is. He'd never admit he framed you."

164

"I'll kill him if he doesn't," Morgan said.

"Oh, that's crazy!" Jean stamped her foot. "Hang for murder? What good would that do you? You heard the sheriff say he didn't believe you robbed the bank. He doesn't like Lamar any better than you do. Nobody does any more. Lamar hasn't got a friend in this town. Even if you came to trial, no jury would convict you."

"Then they wouldn't convict me if I killed him," Morgan said. "They'd probably build me a statue in front of the court-house."

He wheeled away from her, not as sure of himself as he wanted Jean to believe. He couldn't think past the fact that Lamar had framed him, and Lamar was the one man who could clear him. He wouldn't have to kill him. All he had to do was to make Lamar *think* he was going to kill him.

He paused at the back door and turned to look at Jean, who was watching him with troubled eyes. She said: "Come back when you get done with Lamar. I won't go to bed. I certainly couldn't sleep if I did."

Morgan nodded, and left the house. He crossed the back yard in long, quick strides and stopped in the shadow of the barn, wondering if Smith and the others had slipped back after leaving and were waiting for him. He didn't think so. He was reasonably sure that Smith knew he was in the bedroom and was listening to the conversation. He probably was counting on Morgan's believing what he and Tully said.

He had to play his hand out, he told himself. He had been telling himself that for quite a while, he thought sourly, but it seemed he had no choice. If Smith and the others were waiting for him, he'd shoot his way past them. That wouldn't help the situation, but again he told himself he had no choice.

He ran down the alley, keeping in the shadows, stopping to listen and look, and then go on. When he reached the rear of the Lamar house, he stopped, seeing that there was a light in one of the back rooms. This surprised him. He had supposed Lamar would be asleep in bed. He could be sure of one thing, he told himself wryly. Lamar's conscience wouldn't be keeping him awake.

Morgan hesitated for a moment, the thought crossing his mind that Molly might be the one who was up and he didn't want to see her, but he wasn't going to worry about that. It was a chance he was willing to take. He ran to the back porch, crossed it to the door, and knocked. A moment later he heard footsteps, then the door opened, and Molly stood there peering at him.

The light in the hall that fell through the open door behind Molly was very thin and it took her a moment to recognize him. He couldn't see her clearly, standing as she was with her back to the light, but it couldn't be anyone else except Molly.

"I want to see . . . ," Morgan began.

"Morgan," she squealed. "Oh, Morgan, I'm so happy to see you. Come in."

She pushed the screen door back and he stepped in, then she threw herself at him, her arms coming around him. She lifted her mouth for his kiss. When he made no effort to kiss her, she reached up and pulled his head down. This was the last thing he had expected and wanted, then he was glad she did it because her lips that had been so warm and exciting did nothing to him now. He knew beyond doubt that the spell she had cast upon him was completely broken.

She gave no indication that she noticed his lack of response. She took his hand that was nearest to her and squeezed it, then said: "Come on back into my sitting room, Morgan. I want to look at you. It's been so long."

She led him along the hall and into her sitting room, then

166

turned and gazed intently at his face. She said, smiling: "You look good to me. I can't tell you how good. I have never felt so deserted and alone as I do tonight. I needed to see you. Dick's gone to the Rafter D to see Armand and your sister, and he left me here by myself. He's leaving the country and expects me to go with him. I don't have the slightest intention of doing anything of the kind, but then, if you hadn't come, I might have done it." She motioned to a nearby chair, sat down, and picked up her embroidery. "Sit down, Morgan. We've got so much to talk about. First I want you to know that I was absolutely stupid to let you leave the country without me and to marry Dick. He's been a truly terrible husband. Compared to you, he just isn't much man."

He sat down and looked at her. Apparently she expected him to pick up where he'd left off, to forgive her for what she had done to him, and to marry her as soon as she divorced Lamar, and that, he thought bitterly, was unrealistic and completely stupid. He sat on the front of the chair, his back stiff, and tried to decide what to say to her.

"Did your husband tell you about him claiming that I robbed his bank?" Morgan said after a moment's silence.

"Oh, yes." She glanced up, smiling. "But I know you didn't do it. He framed you and he told me he had. I'll tell the sheriff if you're worried about it. It was silly. No one would believe what Dick said. He's a chronic liar, you know. I guess that's no news to you."

He took a long breath of relief. "I'm glad to know that you'll clear me. I've been worried."

"You shouldn't be," she said reassuringly. "I don't think Dick believes he'll succeed in blaming you for the bank's money being gone. Anyhow, he knows he's finished in Twin Rocks, so he went out to get five thousand dollars from Armand, and then he's leaving."

"How can he get five thousand out of Buck Armand?" Morgan asked.

"He said he had a paper you had signed giving up your claim to the Rafter D," she said. "I guess he must have been telling the truth or he wouldn't have ridden out to the ranch. I mean, he just doesn't like to ride that well, but I didn't believe you'd sign any paper like that and throw away your share of the property that's rightfully yours."

"Let's say he tricked me," Morgan said.

He had been staring at her, thinking she had changed a great deal in the time he had been gone. He had trouble deciding what the change was. She was not as pretty as he remembered her. She looked much older, with lines of discontent around her eyes. He guessed that was the biggest change. Some people seem not to be changed by time, but Molly Lamar was not one of them.

"Well, I know one thing," she said. "Dick will go to prison if he doesn't get away, or if he can't prove to Smith that you're the one who robbed the bank. If I tell the sheriff what I know, then I guess he will go to prison, won't he?"

She was making herself plain enough, he thought. She was really saying that, if he wanted her, she could clear him. He rose, telling himself that if it came to bargaining like that, he'd take his chances surrendering to Ed Smith.

She threw the embroidery down and jumped up as Morgan said: "I'll stop by later and see Lamar."

"No!" she cried. "He won't be here more than a minute when he stops to get me. You'll miss him. He'll want me to go with him and I'll tell him I'm not going, and then he'll leave. He'll have to. Don't you see, Morgan? I'll tell him plain out that I'll testify for you. I'll tell the sheriff what he told me. That's all it'll take to clear you, isn't it?"

He shook his head. "He'd swear you were lying. It would

168

be better if I got a confession out of him."

He backed toward the door. She said in a frantic tone: "Morgan, please stay here till he comes. I'm afraid of what he'll do to me if I don't go with him. After he leaves, I'll go with you to the sheriff's house and we'll get him out of bed and I'll tell him."

He found it hard to believe that Molly thought she could roll back the years this way and go right on as they had when he was so much in love with her that he didn't have a thought for anything or anyone else. Yet that certainly was what she was thinking, but, then, she never had been realistic. To her the world had always been what she wanted it to be.

"It won't work, Molly," he said brusquely. "We can't pick up where we left off."

He wheeled toward the door, hearing her cry out: "Yes, we can, Morgan! Let me show you that we can!"

He was in the hall by then. He kept going, across the porch and the back yard. Without thought he turned toward Jean's house, feeling empty and frustrated. Molly wouldn't testify for him unless he bowed to her every whim.

He still had to see Lamar. It was his only chance, but if Molly was telling the truth about the banker's leaving town, there was small chance he would find the man. On the other hand, he wasn't staying here until Lamar showed up. Right now all he wanted to do was to put some distance between himself and Molly.

XVII

Lamar tied his horse in front of the Rafter D ranch house, noting that there was a light in the front room, so some of them were up. He was glad. He didn't want to waste time pounding on the door and waiting for Armand to get dressed. The sooner he got this over with and started back to town the better.

He walked up the path to the front door, uneasiness beginning to work through him. He hadn't felt it before because his mind had been on Molly and his slide from the pinnacle of respectability into poverty and oblivion. A few months after he had left Twin Rocks no one would remember him unless they blamed him for the bank's going under. He would just as soon that they forgot him as to remember him that way.

He crossed the porch and knocked, not sure why this sudden fit of uneasiness had struck him unless it was the simple truth that Buck Armand was a hard and unpredictable man to deal with. He was given to terrible fits of temper, and, if he thought of something to blame Lamar for, the next few minutes were going to be hell.

Celia opened the door, saw who it was, and said with cold contempt: "Oh, it's you, Lamar. Come in."

No respect for him, Lamar thought bitterly as he stepped into the living room. There had been a time not so long ago when no one, not even Celia Armand, would have thought of addressing him as anything but Mr. Lamar. Slowly and insidiously this respect that a community naturally holds for its banker had eroded until it no longer existed. To hell with it, he thought sourly as he nodded at Armand who was sitting on a battered leather couch. He wouldn't be around very much longer to think about minor things such as his

170

fading dignity and respect.

"Howdy, Buck," he said.

Armand gave him a bare half-inch nod, not taking the trouble to speak. Uneasiness grew in Lamar and spread down into his belly like a paralyzing liquid that froze his insides. Armand was in an evil mood. His battered face looked as if he had tangled with a grizzly, but Lamar decided it would be a mistake to ask what had happened.

"Morgan Dill's back," Lamar said.

"We know it," Armand grunted. "Did you get the paper?"

Lamar nodded. "It worked just as we planned. He didn't like the notion of signing the paper, but my gun was a powerful persuader."

"All right, all right," Armand said impatiently. "Let's have the paper."

"It's right here." Lamar patted his coat pocket. "Let's see the money."

"You think you're going to get the money before I see the paper?" Armand demanded. "You're crazy. For all I know you may have forged his signature."

"I'll know it," Celia said. "I've seen Morgan's handwriting often enough."

Lamar looked from Armand's bruised face to Celia's fat one with the drooping jowl. In all of his life, he told himself, he had never seen two more disagreeable people. The uneasiness had turned to fear as he decided he'd give them the paper and take his money and get out. He reached into his coat and drew out the folded sheet of paper. He handed it to Celia.

"Look at the signature all you want to," he said. "It's his, all right. Maybe a little shaky, him sitting there under my gun when he signed, but it's his."

Celia held the paper close to the lamp and studied it a

moment. She nodded as she handed it to her husband. "It's Morgan's, all right."

Armand gave a quick glance. He said: "I'm satisfied if Celia is."

Armand sat motionlessly. Celia moved away from him toward the stand in the middle of the room and stood staring at Lamar. The banker looked from one to the other and back. Neither showed any intention of going after the money. The horrible fear raced through his mind that they weren't going to give it to him.

"Where's my five thousand?" Lamar demanded.

"What five thousand?" Armand asked with bland innocence.

"By God, you're not weaseling out of it. I made an agreement with both of you and I kept my part. I expect you to keep yours."

Armand shrugged his thick shoulders. "You can expect what you damn' please."

"If you don't give it to me," Lamar threatened, "I'll tell the whole plan to Smith."

"Go ahead," Armand said. "You'll be in the jug with us."

Sweat began pouring down Lamar's face. He took a handkerchief from his pocket and wiped his face. He asked hoarsely: "You're refusing to give me the money?"

"I've got a convenient memory," Armand said. "Right now I can't remember making any agreement with you that's concerned with five thousand dollars. You wanted an arrangement that covered your own thievery, and this deal with Morgan was just what you needed. That's profit enough for you. Now you can walk out of here and look Ed Smith in the face and you'll know he can't touch you. Otherwise, you'd be headed for Canon City. I guess the pen down there ain't so bad, but I don't think you'd like it, being used to all the comforts you are."

The bald-faced effrontery turned Lamar's fear into anger. He found it hard to believe that Armand was serious, but there was no trace of humor in the broad, bruised face. Only cold contempt. The anger grew until it turned into rage. He began to tremble.

"I've got to have the money," Lamar said in a tight voice. "I'm leaving town and there's nothing left in the bank. I gave all the cash that was in the safe to Dill. I counted on your keeping your word. I've got to have a stake when I leave here. I won't walk out of this house until I get it."

"Oh, you'll be walking out pretty soon," Armand said, "if you're able to walk. I'm riding out and I sure ain't leaving you here with my pretty wife. So why don't you just get on your horse and ride back to town?"

Lamar thought about Molly and how he had promised her he'd have $5,000. She would never leave with him unless he had it. She had no respect for a man who was broke. He had a chance to regain her respect if he had money; he had no chance whatever if he didn't have any.

He didn't move. All the fear and uneasiness was gone from him now. In its place was a cold fury such as he had never known before in his life. He rubbed his hands up and down against his pants legs; he felt the weight of the gun and a compelling urge to reach for it swelled up in him. Armand's hands were palms down on his thighs. They looked swollen. If they were, Armand would have trouble handling his gun.

"Armand," Lamar said slowly, "you'd better know something before you make up your mind to cheat me. I've gone downhill until I've reached the bottom. The money you owe me is all I've got coming from anyone. I know you've got it. You withdrew more than that a few days ago. I tell you I'm going to have it if I have to kill you."

"Give it to him," Celia said wearily. "He's right. We made an agreement."

Armand was on his feet, a malicious grin tugging at the corners of his swollen mouth. He said: "You couldn't kill me if I gave you the first five shots. You just don't have the guts, banker man. If you had, you wouldn't be where you are, yelling about being broke and begging me for money. No, Celia, I won't give it to him. Look at him, shaky and scared so he's turned white. Or maybe it's green. I guess a man turns green when he's scared, don't he?"

"Give it to him and get him out of here," Celia said. "He makes me sick just looking at him."

"Yeah, he makes me sick, too," Armand said. "Mosey on out of here before I throw up."

It was bad enough to have a promise broken and not get the money that was due him; it was worse to be insulted after he had done exactly what he had bargained to do. It was unfair and wrong, but there was no use to go on begging. He knew Armand well enough to be sure that he would not change his mind. Still, knowing that, he continued to beg.

"You don't understand," he said, so tired he found it hard to make the words come. "You see, I've got to have that money. Molly won't go with me unless I do and she's got to go. That means you've got to give it to me. I'll say please and get down on my knees and do any damned thing you want me to do. Just keep your promise."

Armand looked at him, his lips curled in disgust. "Get out, banker. Go back to town and look in your safe. Maybe a few nickels are left for a man who will say please and get down on his knees."

Lamar took a long breath as all self-control left him. What he did was not the result of a cool, rational decision. It was simply the reflex action of a man who knew there was nothing left for him if he walked out of this house empty-handed. The thumb of his right hand was hooked under his waistband. Now he jerked it out and wrapped his hand around the butt of the gun and lifted it from leather.

Armand's first bullet struck him in the chest and knocked him down. It was like the blow of a sledge-hammer. He couldn't breathe; he knew he had dropped his gun and his hand began searching for it. He had heard the roar of the shot; he had heard Celia's scream, and now Armand's brutal face seemed to be detached from his beefy shoulders and was floating in space in front of him, then the Colt roared again and Dick Lamar saw and heard nothing more.

"You idiot!" Celia screamed. "You didn't have to kill the little weasel. All you had to do was to take his gun away from him. I never saw a man make a slower draw in my life. You could have walked over to him and taken the gun away from him before he pulled the trigger."

Armand shoved his gun back into the holster. "Maybe I could have," he said. "Maybe not. I reckon it don't make any difference, but I liked the notion of fixing it so his mouth was shut for good. Now he won't be making no deal with Smith and telling him how he got the idea of framing Morgan." For just a moment Armand stared at the motionless body. He said—"No guts."—and started toward the front door.

XVIII

Celia stood motionlessly, her gaze on Lamar's body. At first she had been stunned, then angry, and now she was furious. She was used to violence, she had seen men killed, but this had been so unnecessary. She'd had no use for the banker, for he had been a willing tool from the beginning. Still, he was in no way a threat to Buck or her. He had been too deeply involved in hers and Buck's plotting to talk. There had simply been no good reason for killing him.

Armand had almost reached the front door when she said: "Buck."

He stopped, then turned slowly. "What the hell do you want?"

"I said you were an idiot," she said. "Well, you're worse. You're a god-damned fool. You didn't accomplish anything by killing Lamar. All you did was to complicate our situation. What are you going to do with the body? How are you going to explain his killing to the sheriff?"

"Do whatever you want to with the body," he said. "It's your problem. I'll leave him here with you."

"No you don't!" she shouted. "I didn't kill him. You did. Now get rid of him."

He shrugged, started to say something, then decided against it, and shut his mouth. Once more he turned toward the door. Celia screamed: "I asked you what you're going to say to the sheriff! Now you'd better tell me because he may ride out here again."

Once more he turned to face her. "We don't need to explain nothing to the star toter."

"If he shows up here again and finds the body, we can't just. . . ."

176

"Say it was an accident."

"He wouldn't believe that," she said scornfully. "And another thing. You're a damned crook as well as an idiot. We did make a bargain with Lamar. It was easier and smarter to keep it than to kill him. What the hell is the matter with you?"

"You're a bigger idiot than I am," he said harshly. "Anybody would be an idiot to give that tinhorn five thousand dollars. You're a good one to call me a crook. I guess a woman who would do all you've done to cheat your brother out of his share of the spread is as big a crook as anyone could be."

"You were in it from the beginning!" she cried. "It was your idea. You were the one who went to Lamar. . . ."

"Oh, shut up." He walked slowly toward her, his fists clenched. "I've had all of your caterwauling I can stomach. You're nothing but a fat old sow who married me because you wanted a man. You'd have done anything to get a husband, only nobody but me was fool enough to take the bait."

"Don't call me a fat old sow!" she shrieked, her face red. "I'm not a nothing as long as the Rafter D is mine. I've always kept my word and my father always kept his. You're the one who's a nothing. A chiseler and a murderer. That's what you are. Now get off my ranch."

He stood very close to her. Suddenly he laughed. "You think you can order me off this spread? You think for a minute the crew would take orders from you? Well, now, that makes you the real idiot. No, you can't get rid of me by ordering me off the ranch." He scratched his chin, his eyes narrowing thoughtfully. "But maybe I'd better get rid of you."

She stared at him, the fury in her giving way to terror. She read murder in his face, cold, premeditated murder, the fulfilling of a plan that had long been in his mind. Then she lost all control and struck him on the side of the face, a hard blow that rocked his head. She had lost her ability to reason, but the instant she hit him, instinct told her she had done the wrong thing, that she was likely to trigger the killing hunger that was in him. She whirled away and tried to run, but he caught her before she reached the kitchen door. He yanked her around and hit her in the belly as he would have hit a man.

Breath was knocked out of her, making a strange wheezing sound. She was on the floor, although she had no memory of falling. She had a crazy feeling that time was suspended, that she was floating and turning in the air. She could not breathe; she had a terrible feeling that she was paralyzed.

Armand stood rubbing his knuckles as he looked down at her. He said: "Later, my good wife. Later."

This time, when he turned to the front door, he kept going. Celia still could not move, but breath was beginning to come back into her lungs now, very slowly and very painfully. She was conscious, yet she couldn't move.

She heard Armand ride away. With a clarity of vision that shocked her, she realized she had been very close to death, that she had been spared only because killing her had not fitted Armand's timing. She had long suspected that he had murdered her father. Now, after seeing Armand gun down Lamar and then stare at her with the naked lust to kill so plainly written on his face, she knew beyond any doubt that he had murdered Abe Dill, that he was moving along a carefully schemed line, and he was intent on keeping everything in perfect order. Her murder would come later after Morgan had been disposed of. She had to leave before he returned or he would kill her even if it wasn't the proper moment.

She discovered she was able to move. Slowly she got to her feet, breath coming easier now. She sat down on the couch and wiped sweat from her face. Her belly hurt, not only from the blow Armand had given her, but from the fear that was like a cold stone in her abdomen. She had been afraid of

Armand before, but not like this. His mask was off at last; for the first time she had seen the real Buck Armand, a man her father had trusted but had never really known.

For a moment she thought about Abe Dill, the man his neighbors had called Lucifer Dill. She understood why. He had always been a brutal and grasping man, one who had simply bulldozed others out of his way until he had gained his objective, but she had never known him to break his word, to fail to keep a promise. Now, staring at Lamar's stiffening body, she was ashamed. She told herself that Buck Armand had brought himself to the lowest possible point that a human being could and in spite of herself she was a part of it.

She knew, then, what she would do. A shiver slid along her spine. For some illogical reason she had a feeling she would not live until morning, an insight that brought cold sweat breaking through her skin. She didn't know how she would die, or at whose hands, but one thing must be done first. Buck Armand had to hang for killing Dick Lamar. She would see that he did. Somewhere along the line she had to clear Morgan. Not that she had suddenly discovered any real love for her brother. It was simply a matter of getting at her husband. If by any chance she lived through the night, she would need Morgan's help.

She rose and left the house, walking slowly and bent forward at the hips. One hand was held against her belly. When she reached the barn, she lighted a lantern and harnessed a team. Leading the horses out of the runway, she hooked them to the buckboard, and drove to the front of the house.

Celia wasn't sure that she could do what she had to do. Her belly had never hurt like this in her entire life and she began to wonder if Armand's blow had damaged her insides. Maybe that was why she had this crazy premonition of death. It was a new sensation to her. She had never really thought much about dying. She had always been a strong, dominating woman who had been able to shape life the way she wanted it, but now her world had slid out from under her.

All the time she had thought she was using Armand, he had actually been using her, working steadily and patiently toward his goal. To him she had been nothing more than the fat old sow he had called her. He must have hated her all this time with a passion, she thought bitterly. He probably had been filled with disgust every time he had touched her.

Slowly she got out of the buckboard and walked into the house, still moving in that painful, bent-over position. Normally she could have picked Lamar up and carried him to the rig, but she knew she couldn't do that now. She blew out the lamp, then took hold of the banker's feet and pulled him through the front door to the porch. She stopped to rest, panting and holding her belly, then went on to the buckboard, the head of the corpse hitting each step with a dull *thwacking* sound as she pulled the body off the porch.

When she reached the buckboard, she had to stop again to rest. The pain was worse now, a deep, stabbing pain that was like a knife thrust deeply into her abdomen. Somehow she had to get the corpse into the buckboard, but that required a straight lift and she couldn't do it.

She wiped her face with a sleeve. When she thought about Armand coming back with his crew and finding her here, she knew she could lift the body regardless of the pain. She stooped, slipped her hands under his shoulders and legs, and lifted him into the buckboard, and then nearly fainted from the pain. For a time she clung to a wheel, tears running down her cheeks. Each breath sent a deeper thrust of pain into her belly than she had felt. She knew with a greater certainty than before that she would die tonight and death was better than living if she had to suffer like this.

She did not know how long she remained that way, her hands clutching the wheel, her eyes closed, the tears running down her face and leaving their salty taste in her mouth. Time was not normal seconds and minutes to her, but seemed to run on and on like an endless river. She remembered when she had been very sick one time with scarlet fever and had almost died, and it had seemed to her that each feverish minute had been an hour. It was that way now.

She couldn't stay here no matter how much she hurt. Help was in town, not on the Rafter D. Slowly she eased into the seat. Taking the lines, she drove across the moon-lighted yard and started down the road toward Twin Rocks.

Yes, she would see to it that Buck Armand died with a rope on his neck for the murder of Dick Lamar. She must survive the night, she told herself, and then she would live a long time, for Buck would not be around to murder her.

XIX

Ed Smith tied his horse in front of the courthouse, stepped up on the boardwalk, and waited for Tully and Johnny Bedlow to dismount and tie. The courthouse was an ugly frame building that needed paint. Now it loomed ahead of him, a gaunt ungainly shape in the moonlight. The yard showed no pretense of a lawn, but held a splendid growth of dog fennel and various other weeds.

Whenever Ed stopped to think about it, the neglect that the county showed the courthouse seemed to him to be indicative of the feeling that the local people had for the law. The courthouse was a symbol of the law. The influence the Rafter D exerted on the law was one reason for that feeling, and it would exist as long as the Rafter D ran the county. Tonight, Ed told himself grimly, that influence would end.

No one had said a word on the way back from Jean Runyan's house. Now Tully stepped up on the boardwalk to stand beside Ed. He asked: "Think he'll come in?"

"Damned if I know," Ed answered. "You can come nearer telling me than I can tell you."

"He was in that bedroom," Tully said thoughtfully. "I'd bet on it, so he heard all we said. I think he'll come in after he's thought about it a while. Trouble is he may be too late."

Johnny joined them, and they walked around the corner of the courthouse to the jail, a small, stone building on the west side of the courthouse. Ed went in first, lighted a lamp, and sat down in his swivel chair at his spur-scarred desk. It was an ancient piece of furniture that went back to the day the courthouse and jail were built and that was a long time ago. Ed had often thought about asking for a new desk and chair, but he

182

hadn't because he knew it would be a waste of time. Asking for anything that required tax money was a waste of time.

"It's gonna be a long wait," Tully grumbled. "I wish to hell Morg would come in. At least, we'd have him to talk to."

"Won't be long," Johnny Bedlow said. "Ain't more'n two, three hours till daylight, then we'll have plenty of excitement."

"We will for a fact," Tully agreed somberly.

Ed glanced at the metal door that opened into the corridor that divided one big cell from two small ones. The jail was empty as it usually was except on Saturday nights when Ed normally picked up a few drunks and held them here until they sobered up.

Ed's duties were seldom demanding. He guessed that more had happened tonight of a lawless nature than in all the previous time he had carried the star. It was a wonder he had been allowed enough money to pay one deputy. He thought moodily that he'd have a job getting Johnny's wages for the time he had put in tonight.

His gaze went on around the office to the gun rack near the door, to the calendar on the wall that pictured a girl in a very short dress. It was a disgrace to the county, Judge Alcorn grumbled, and Ed remembered replying sourly that, if the judge didn't like the scenery here, he could go back to his own office. Several Reward dodgers yellowed by age were tacked to the wall beside the calendar, all showing outlaws' fierce, mustached faces. Chances were every one of them was dead or in jail somewhere.

He rose and paced the length of his office and back. He couldn't stand it here another minute. He said: "I'm going home for a little while. Mary's probably sitting up, worrying about me."

"Go ahead," Tully said, still grumpy. "I wish I had a wife

who was sitting up, worrying about me."

"Especially a pretty one like Mary," Johnny said, grinning. "You're a lucky man, Ed."

"I figure I am," Ed agreed.

He looked at Tully, who didn't meet his gaze. He had seldom seen his deputy in a mood as low as this. He understood how Tully felt about Morgan Dill, how much pressure Tully had been under all evening. He said: "I think he'll come in, Tully. You might as well quit worrying."

"Hell, I ain't worryin'," Tully snapped. "I'm as happy as the first robin in spring. I just wish it was sunup and I had my sights on that god-damned Buck Armand."

"He'll be here soon enough," Ed said, and left the jail.

He mounted and rode to his house, thinking how uneventful the months had been since he had taken the star. He had never been forced to face a tough situation before, at least against odds like this. Oh, he'd gone after wanted men and brought them in, but that wasn't facing the Rafter D crew.

The fact was he had never really been tested. Well, he'd be tested before this was over, he told himself sourly, and admitted that he would feel better if Morgan was in the jail with them. Funny thing, he thought, as he strode up the path to the front door. He was supposed to arrest Morgan Dill, and yet he was thinking that he needed Morgan because he was a fighting man, and Ed had mentally leaned on him ever since he'd heard what Buck Armand planned to do.

He opened the front door and stepped into the living room. A lamp was burning on the oak stand in the middle of the room. He saw that Mary was curled up on the couch, an afghan pulled over her. She stirred as he crossed the room to her and sat up and yawned.

"Must be two o'clock," she said.

He nodded. "About."

184

"Ed, did you find the Dill boy?"

He shook his head as he drew up a chair and sat down beside her. "We know where he is, or think we do. We hope he'll turn himself in. We could have gone after him, but some of us would have been dead, if we had."

"You're learning." She reached out and took his hand. "I'm glad."

He knew what was in her mind. She had often accused him of rushing into a situation before he looked. He winked at her as he said: "Give me credit."

"Oh, I do. I do."

"I don't suppose you've slept any tonight."

"Not much," she admitted. "Tell me what's happened."

He told her, adding: "Armand might be bluffing, but I've played poker with him and I found out he ain't a bluffer. He waits until he's got the power, then he tears you apart. I think he'll play this hand the same way."

"How many men will he bring?"

"I don't know. Maybe ten. Maybe twelve."

"And there's three of you?"

"Four, if Morgan Dill turns himself in. He'll fight with us. The thing is he may not make up his mind in time to be of any help."

They sat in silence for a time, holding hands and being very much aware that these minutes might be the last they would spend together. Presently Mary said: "Remember the time we rode up to Coogan's Falls and the storm caught us and we had to stay there all night?"

He laughed. "How could I forget it? Your dad dusted off his shotgun when we got back. If it hadn't been for that, I don't think we'd ever have had the courage to tell him we were getting married."

She nodded, smiling as old memories came back to her.

She said: "We've had a good life, Ed, and I've been a very happy woman. I don't envy anyone in this whole, wide world."

"Not even Molly Lamar in her fine big house?"

"Molly least of all."

"I ain't looking forward to getting killed," Ed said somberly, "but it ain't so much that I'm afraid to die that bothers me. I'd never have run for sheriff if I felt that way. What worries me the most is that I've helped bring some children into the world and I want to help raise them. I won't leave you very well fixed, either."

She squeezed his hand. "Don't worry. Not for a minute. Sure, it'll be hard, but I'm young and strong and I'll make out." Then in spite of herself she began to cry. "I'm sorry." She wiped her eyes and shook her head. "I didn't aim to do that. It's just that I love you so much that I can't even bring myself to think how it would be if you weren't here."

He rose. "We're borrowing trouble and there's no sense in that. Maybe I'll make out all right."

She stood up, her head tipped back, worried eyes on him. She asked: "You think Armand actually will burn the town if he doesn't find Morgan Dill?"

"I think Buck Armand is crazy enough to do anything," Ed said. "He stood in old Abe's shadow for a long time and now he figures on making his own shadow. He's going to be damned sure that he throws a longer one than Abe ever did. If it comes to that, get the kids out of the house. You'd better get them clear out of town."

"I'll take care of them," she said. "Don't worry about us."

She put her arms around him and hugged him hard, then tipped her head back for his kiss. "I'm proud of you, Ed. I never knew how proud until tonight. Some men would have had business elsewhere."

He nodded, remembering how Caleb Mason, who had carried the star for years, always said that time would solve anything and he made it a habit to go fishing when anything that threatened danger loomed ahead.

He kissed her, her lips sweet and warm. He ran a hand down her back and patted her behind. "Go to bed, honey. No use wasting the whole night."

She shook her head. "I'll keep my clothes on and stay here on the couch. Send for me if you need me."

He nodded and turned away quickly, not wanting her to see his expression. When he was outside, he blew his nose and swallowed, wondering if anyone ever found security in this life. He guessed not. Security wasn't a part of man's heritage on earth.

Mounting, he rode back to the courthouse. He dismounted and for a while stood on the boardwalk, his head cocked, listening, but he heard nothing. It wasn't time yet and he wondered why he had stopped to listen for Rafter D's approach. Maybe his nerves were beginning to crack. If he could meet a danger head-on, he could handle it, but waiting had always been hell for him.

When he went into the jail, Tully and Johnny Bedlow were playing cards. He asked: "Anything happen?"

"Not a thing," Tully answered.

"Quiet as a tomb," Johnny added.

Tully scowled at him. "Now that's a hell of a thing to say."

"Ain't it now?" Johnny agreed. "I'll change it. This is a good night for murder."

"Oh, for God's sake," Tully growled.

Ed sat down at his desk, thinking that Johnny's attempt at humor had failed. There was nothing to do now but wait.

XX

Morgan returned to Jean Runyan's house after he left Molly
Lamar because he didn't know where else to go or what to do.
He felt trapped. He wanted nothing from Molly. He never
wanted to see her again, but he'd have to if he went back to force
a confession out of Dick Lamar.

As he crossed the yard to Jean's back door, he asked himself again if Molly had been lying about her husband's leaving
town. If she was telling the truth, just how bad did he want to
get that admission of guilt out of Lamar? He honestly didn't
know. Maybe Lamar wouldn't admit anything regardless of
what Morgan did to him. Maybe he'd been foolish to come
back to town. He was tempted to saddle up and ride away and
say to hell with all of it. He knew at once he could not. He had
never ridden away from anything and he wasn't starting now.

Well, he'd talk to Jean, if she was still awake, drink another
cup of coffee, and wind up going back to the Lamar house.
Perhaps he could catch the banker outside. Anyhow, he
shouldn't let Molly get to him the way he had. He didn't
know why it had happened. He was certain he no longer loved
her; he knew he was far better off the way it had turned out. It
was just that seeing her and having her throw herself at him
brought back all the old dreams that were broken, dreams
that had been good at the time, but now seemed childish.
More than that, it had hurt him to see Molly trample on her
pride and beg him to take her back. She had been a proud
woman. Now all she could think of was to jump from one man
who could no longer take care of her to a man who could.

He stepped into the kitchen and stopped, his hand dropping to his gun. Someone was with Jean in the front room.

For a moment he stood motionlessly, trying to place the man's voice and failing, then Jean called: "That you, Morgan?"

He didn't answer. He eased across the kitchen, staying close to the wall so he could not be seen by anyone who was in the other room. He heard Jean say: "I was sure someone came in. I'll go see."

He stepped through the doorway, his gun in his hand. He said: "It's me, all right." Then he stopped, breathing hard, his gun lined on the man. It was Judge Alcorn.

"Well, by God, Jean," he said in a low tone as if he could not believe what he saw. "You sold me out. You set a trap for me."

"I did no such thing," she said angrily.

"Don't tell me the judge just wandered over here at this time of night because he couldn't sleep. You knew I'd be back, so you went after him, didn't you?"

"Yes, I did," she said resentfully. "Sometimes you act as if you don't know who your friends are, Morgan Dill. You're so stubborn you don't even think straight. All I wanted was to get you to talk to the judge. Now sit down and talk while I get the coffee."

"It really isn't much of a trap, is it, Morgan?" the judge said. "You've got the gun on me. I sure don't have one on you."

Morgan looked down at the gun in his hand, then raised his gaze to Alcorn's face. He had forgotten how old and frail the judge was. Or perhaps Alcorn had aged more in the three years Morgan had been gone than he normally would have. In any case he had nothing to fear from Judge Alcorn. Liver spots covered the backs of his claw-like hands. His thin face was as deeply lined as the last apple in the barrel late in spring. Suddenly Morgan was ashamed. He had been going on the basis that he could not trust anybody. Maybe Jean was right. He guessed he didn't know who his friends were.

He holstered his gun and held his hand out to Alcorn. "Seems like I was out of line, Judge. Will you shake hands?"

"Of course, I'll shake hands." Alcorn rose and gripped Morgan's hand, his gaze boring into the younger man's face. "You went away a boy, Morgan, and now I've got to quit thinking of you as a boy. You came back a man. I'm glad to see you. I'm hoping you'll be our ally. We need one."

Morgan remembered what Tully and Ed Smith had said about needing him and his gun, and now Judge Alcorn was saying the same thing.

"I don't savvy this, Judge," Morgan said. "Tully and the sheriff were here a while ago trying to soft-soap Jean into talking me into giving myself up. They claimed they'd be needing me, that Buck Armand was bringing the Rafter D to town to find me and hang me for horse stealing, and they'd burn the town if they didn't find me. It sounded like hogwash to me."

"It's no hogwash. I would put nothing past Buck Armand." Alcorn motioned toward a chair. "Sit down, Morgan. I've got some things to say to you and I want you to listen. That's why I got out of bed to talk to you."

Jean came in with the coffee. Morgan took a cup and sat down. "I guess I jumped the gun, Jean," he said. "I'm sorry."

"You ought to be," she snapped. "I'm getting tired of trying to help a man who won't be helped. If you're not going to listen to the judge, then I'll quit trying to help you."

He sipped his coffee, quick rebellion boiling up in him. They didn't know, he told himself. He was the one who had been framed. He was the one who had looked into the muzzle of Lamar's gun. He was the one who had fought for his life with Buck Armand. He was the one whose sister had hit him over the head and knocked him cold. He was the one Ed Smith wanted to lock up in his stinking jail. Well, he'd listen, and then he'd get up and walk out. To hell with Jean. If she didn't want to help him, then he sure didn't want her help.

"I had called a meeting in my office before we knew you were back in town," Alcorn said. "Sam Colter and Baldy Miles were there along with Ed Smith. I guess folks think that Colter and Miles and me kind of run things in Twin Rocks. We did, I suppose, years ago, but we don't any more. I hate like hell to admit this, but we're all scared. Well, we were talking about your coming back, seeing as your birthday is coming up now, and we agreed that you and Johnny Bedlow and Tully Bean had been pretty harum-scarum when you were boys, but we've seen Johnny and Tully settle down. Tully's a deputy and a good one. Johnny's got his barbershop and he's doing fine. We figured you'd settle down, too, when you got back."

Rebellion was still high in Morgan. He said angrily: "I came back with the idea of getting a decent deal out of Celia. As far as settling down is concerned, I'd like to, but all I got was a frame-up from your honest banker."

"I know," Alcorn said quickly. "Jean has been telling me what happened tonight. I don't believe for a minute that you held up the bank."

"Ed Smith does," Morgan snapped, "and he's the one who's looking for me."

Alcorn shook his head. "Ed doesn't believe it, either. It's just that he's got to hold you till this is cleared up. You see, none of us trusts Lamar. We've been worried about him for quite a while, but we didn't know what to do. Of course, we never dreamed he'd work a deal with Celia and Armand, and that's exactly what he'd done. I'm sure of it."

"What happened at Lamar's house when you went over?" Jean asked.

Morgan told her, adding: "Maybe I never really knew Molly. Not the way you did, living with her and growing up with her and all, but I still can't believe she used to be like she is now. I couldn't have been that blind."

"She's worse," Jean admitted. "Once she got a taste of Twin Rocks' social life, she wasn't satisfied with anything Lamar did for her. She used to envy the women who were the high mucky-mucks of town, but it wasn't enough when she got to be one."

Morgan shook his head, still not believing that the Molly he had been in love with could have been that foolish, but the Molly he had seen tonight could. They were two different women, and this was the part he could not understand, that the Molly he had loved simply did not exist.

"The part I want you to know," Alcorn said, "is that Lamar's not the problem. Maybe he is the way you see it, but he's not. I think Molly will clear you, if I talk to her, so you don't need to get a confession out of Lamar. I suggest you don't go back there. You might end up killing him, and then you'd have more trouble than we can handle."

"I feel like killing him," Morgan admitted, "but I'm in more trouble now than I can handle if Lamar doesn't clear me. If I don't stick around after Molly, she won't tell the truth."

"I'll get it out of her," Alcorn said. "I'm slow making my point, but what I've been trying to say is that Buck Armand is the dangerous one. You'll remember that your pa was high-handed and hard to get along with. He got what he wanted from the town and we swallowed our pride to give it to him." The judge jabbed a finger at Morgan. "The difference is that Abe Dill was sane and knew where to stop. Armand is crazy and he won't stop at anything once he decides to do it. He wants it all, and I've got a hunch that getting all of it means killing you and Celia. He looks down on any of us who represent the law, and that means he thinks we can't stop him."

"Even if I'm cleared of robbing the bank," Morgan said, "I won't get my share of the Rafter D. I signed a paper. . . ."

"Jean told me," Alcorn interrupted, "but I can assure you that the agreement you signed will not hold up in my court. You signed under duress and that robs it of any legality."

"Well, it still goes back to proving that I'm telling the truth," Morgan said, "so we're right where we started. Judge, I tell you I will not rot in Ed Smith's jail."

"Nobody expects you to," Alcorn said sharply. "Armand's riding high right now. I'm sure he thinks he's got everything in the palm of his hand. One thing he's been up to is to force the small outfits to throw in with him when he makes his drive to the railroad. I'm not sure just what his angle is, but you can be sure he's got one. Another thing is he owes money to both Colter and Miles, but it's plain enough that he doesn't aim to pay either of them. He's making his own law, Morgan. That's why he believes he can come to town and hang you, or burn the town to force you into the open, and nobody will touch him."

"The crew won't stick with him when it comes to something like burning the town," Morgan said.

"You don't know the Rafter D men," Alcorn said. "Not many of them anyhow. He fired most of the hands you knew and hired toughs who will take his orders. Just two or three like Slim Turner are left. He pays better than average wages, so they've got a good deal and they know it." He shook his head. "No, they'll do what he tells them no matter how unreasonable or criminal it is. Maybe Turner and the other old hands won't, but there's not enough of them to change anything."

193

"I don't savvy this," Morgan said. "You don't have any fighting men in town, but you could recruit some of the small ranchers you were mentioning. As I remember it, there's fifteen or twenty little spreads in the county."

"There's not that many now," Alcorn said. "The Rafter D has swallowed some of them and the rest are too scared of Armand to buck him. Anyhow, there isn't time. Armand will be here in another hour or so. You don't seem to savvy that. Your gun could make the difference."

They were watching him, waiting for him to say he would give himself up, that he would fight alongside Ed Smith and his deputies, that he would help save a town that wanted to jail him for a crime he had not committed. That wasn't exactly true about the town wanting to jail him, he admitted to himself. Most of the old and retired people who lived in Twin Rocks did not even know what had happened, but Ed Smith represented the law and he wanted to jail Morgan.

He shook his head. "I'm sorry, Judge. Ed Smith can maybe kill me, but he's not going to lock me up in his lousy jail as long as I'm alive."

XXI

The ride into town was the most agonizing experience in Celia's life. The wheels seemed to find all the bumps and holes in the road and each bounce drove a knife thrust of pain through her abdomen every time she hit bottom. On more than one occasion she thought she would faint. She rode bent forward, one hand holding the lines, the other pressed against her belly.

She reached Twin Rocks before sunup, the first color of dawn showing in the eastern sky. She pulled to a stop in front of the courthouse and for a time sat motionlessly in the seat, her eyes closed, and waiting for the pain to ease off.

In spite of the pain, there seemed to be a startling clarity to her thinking. She had no regrets for what she had done in her life except for one thing. Her mistake had been to marry Buck Armand. She had thought more than once about killing him and now she wished she had. She'd had both means and opportunity. By waiting, she had given him a chance to kill her. She didn't know what the blow he had given her had done to her, but she thought she was dying. It was too bad, she told herself bitterly, to die and leave Buck Armand alive.

Now Morgan would have all of the Rafter D if he lived. If, by some miracle, she did not die, she would own half the ranch and she would need Morgan to run the outfit. She could get along with him if she had to. He was honest. He knew the cattle business. He was a good worker. The truth, then, was plain. Instead of fighting Morgan and trying to cheat him out of his share of the Rafter D and marrying Armand to help achieve her goal, she should have accepted Morgan as a partner and worked with him. It was too late now to live those years over, but, if she didn't die, the

195

future was going to be different.

She eased out of the seat, and then, with her feet on the ground, she had to hold to the side of the buckboard to keep from falling. Maybe she would live, she told herself, live long enough to get rid of Armand, and, if she lived that long, she might keep right on living. Her thoughts focused on her husband. God, how she hated him. She had hated many people in her life, but none the way she hated Buck Armand. Slowly her thoughts turned to Morgan. She would have to convince him that he could get along with her. He must be around here somewhere. She wanted to talk to him. That was strange, too, something she had never dreamed she would want to do.

She gritted her teeth against the spasm of pain. Her head was swimming and the street was turning around like a giant top. She realized then she was not thinking as clearly as she thought she was. Now the only thing she wanted to do was to lie down and not think at all.

She was aware that there were men around her and one was asking: "What's wrong, Missus Armand?"

She recognized Ed Smith in the thin light. Two other men were standing beside him. They'd be Tully Bean and Johnny Bedlow. She said: "Buck hit me in the belly before he left the ranch. I guess he did something bad to my insides. I hurt like hell."

"We'll get you into the jail where you can lie down," Smith said. "Tully, give me a hand."

"Bean, put my rig away," Celia ordered. "The carcass is Dick Lamar. Buck shot and killed him tonight. Get him over to the undertaker."

Tully hesitated, glancing at Smith. The sheriff said: "All right, Tully. Do what she said. Johnny, you can help me."

She was a heavy woman, but somehow they got her into the jail, dragging her more than carrying her. She lay down on

196

one of the bunks in the big cell and closed her eyes. She groaned, gritting her teeth as another spasm of pain struck her.

A moment later, when the worst of the pain had passed, she asked: "Get the doc, Smith. Maybe he can help."

"Doc Bridges is out of town, Missus Armand," Johnny said. "Missus Downey's having her baby."

"Oh, hell, then I've got to lie here and grunt," she muttered. "I guess you know Buck's bringing the crew to town. They'll be along pretty soon. He's bound to get Morgan."

"We're expecting 'em," Smith said.

"He murdered Lamar," Celia said. "Shot him down like a skunk. It was murder, I tell you. You've got to arrest him and hold him for murder."

Smith was silent for a moment, then he said: "All right, Missus Armand, we'll take care of it."

"You'll have a hell of a job doing it," she said. "He'll try to tell you that Lamar had a gun, that it wasn't murder. Well, Lamar had a gun, all right, but he shouldn't have tried to draw. Anybody could have done better. It was murder, all right, same as shooting a baby. Just 'cause he had a gun didn't stop it from being murder."

"Why did he kill Lamar?" Smith asked.

"Lamar wanted money. We'd made a deal. . . ." She stopped, realizing that she had started to incriminate herself. "They had a row. That was all. Lamar lost his head. He tried for his gun, but he never had no chance at all."

She was silent, one hand over her abdomen, her eyes still closed. She groaned in spite of herself and gritted her teeth to keep from groaning again. "My God, it hurts. I'll bet he busted my liver."

"Why did he hit you?" Smith asked.

"We had a row, too," she said. "Over him killing Lamar.

We called each other some names, and finally I lost my temper and hit him. It was a mistake. He can hit harder than I can." She didn't bother to say anything for a time, then she asked: "You don't think Doc will get back pretty soon?"

"I doubt it," Smith said. "The Downeys live 'way up Rock Creek."

"What are we going to do when Buck gets to town?" she asked. "He won't let nothing stop him till he finds and hangs Morgan. You know as well as I do that Morgan can't fight the whole crew."

"We're hoping that Morgan will come in," Smith said. "If he does, the four of us can hold Buck and the boys off. This jail is solid."

"You don't know Buck," she said. "I've lived with him and quarreled with him and slept with him, and, by God, I know him. Morgan's in town, ain't he?"

"Yeah, he's here."

"You know where?"

"We think he's in Jean Runyan's house."

"You think?" She opened her eyes. "Don't you know?"

"Not exactly. We ain't seen him, but we found his horse in Jean's barn, so we figure he's in her house."

"You told him about Buck coming after him?"

"We told Jean. She kept saying he wasn't there, but I'm sure she was lying."

"Morgan's stubborner'n a mule," she said. "Why didn't you bring him in for his own protection?"

"He wouldn't have come," Smith answered. "We figured we'd wind up killing each other if we forced him. What about the bank robbery that Lamar accused Morgan of? You know anything about it?"

"Sure I know about it," she said. "You don't think a Dill would rob a bank, do you?"

"No, but we want to know what did happen?"

"Lamar robbed it hisself," she said, "which same you could have guessed. He's been losing money gambling and the bank was broke, so he comes to Buck with the notion of framing Morgan, figuring that Morgan would come back to Twin Rocks if he had a little push, this being close to his birthday. Buck was to give Lamar five thousand dollars for framing Morgan, but Buck didn't keep his word. That was what made Lamar so mad he pulled his gun."

"So Morgan had nothing to do with it?"

"Hell, no!"

"Will you swear to that in court?"

"If I live that long," she said.

She had finally got around to telling Smith without leaving herself wide open. She'd never tell anyone that she was into the scheme as deeply as Buck was. If the damned fool had only paid Lamar as he had agreed, they wouldn't be in the fix they were now and she could have said to hell with Morgan. Now Buck was coming with his men and they were past the point of working anything out. Morgan had to be kept alive. The only chance of doing that was getting him to come here.

"I want to see Morgan," she said. "Go get him. Tell him I can clear him and he won't be in no more trouble."

"I dunno if he'll come," Smith said.

"Try," she urged. "If you tell him I want to see him to make a reasonable deal for his share of the Rafter D, he'll come."

"All right, Johnny," Smith said. "Go tell him."

Johnny Bedlow left the jail. Smith remained beside the bunk. For a long time Celia lay there, groaning, sweat running down her face. Then she said: "Smith, I aim to kill Buck. Don't arrest me for murder. It'll be an execution. His men won't stand with him. I'm the one who owns the Rafter D and

I pay 'em. I'll remind 'em of that, and then I'm going to kill him."

Smith, still looking down at her, wished it was that simple.

XXII

Morgan sat in Jean Runyan's living room, feeling Jean's and Alcorn's eyes on him. He was uncomfortable, and, in spite of himself, he felt a little guilty. Suppose Buck Armand did come to town with the Rafter D crew and burn every building trying to root him out of his hiding place? It wouldn't happen. He was sure of it, but, if it did, he would feel guiltier than ever. He shifted in his chair, feeling his face get red.

He started to tell them to quit staring at him, that he had a right to make his own decisions whether they were wrong or not, and that he was the one who would rot in the county jail if Ed Smith arrested him. He didn't say any of those things because he heard steps on the porch, and then a man's heavy knock.

Morgan jumped up and drew his gun. He motioned for Jean to answer the knock as he backed into the kitchen. Jean opened the door and said something, then he heard her say: "Come in. Morgan's here."

He swore softly, thinking that it might be Ed Smith and Jean was not going to play the game his way any longer. There was no sense in pretending he wasn't here, so he stepped through the door, his gun still in his hand. Johnny Bedlow stood there, his Colt still in his holster.

"Damn it, Morg," Johnny said testily, "put up that gun. You've set everybody on their ear tonight. It's time you came back down to earth and listened to reason."

Morgan didn't say anything for a moment, the sharp memory of Johnny's refusing to shake hands with him crowding into his mind. Tully was the more opinionated of his two friends, the one who used to give him an argument when they disagreed on anything, but Johnny had always been the easy-going one, so Morgan still could not understand why Johnny had acted the way he had.

Because he hesitated, not speaking and not holstering his gun, Johnny said angrily: "I said put it up. I'm not here to make any trouble for you. My gun's not in my hand, either, but it would have been if I'd intended to take you in. Now, what the hell are you worried about?"

Morgan knew he could outdraw Johnny if it came to that. Johnny had never been one to lie or deceive him, and he didn't think he was now. Slowly he lowered the gun and dropped it into leather. He said: "I was glad to see you when I first got to town, but you weren't glad to see me. Why?"

"You mean why didn't I shake hands with you?" Johnny asked. "Well, I'm sorry I didn't, but the reason wasn't because I wasn't glad to see you. I was scared. I'd heard Buck Armand talk in the barbershop about what he would do to you if you ever came back to Twin Rocks. I didn't expect to see you, and, when I did, all I could think of was to tell Ed Smith. I thought he could protect you."

"I never saw the day I needed to have Ed Smith's protection," Morgan said hotly.

"I know that," Johnny admitted. "I acted on the spur of the moment and I'm sorry I didn't shake hands with you, but I didn't come here to apologize. I came to tell you that your sister is in Ed's office and she wants to see you."

"To hell with her," Morgan said harshly. "She saw me once tonight. She sure didn't act like she wanted to see me then."

"Things have changed," Johnny said. "You'd be a fool if you didn't go, though I reckon you are pretty much of a fool, playing hard to find all night the way you've been doing."

Morgan was tempted to tell him to get out and let him alone, but he hesitated, wondering what had changed. Before he could ask, Jean said: "He had reason to play hard to find, with Ed acting like he believed Lamar's story, but maybe it's time to stop playing that game. What's changed?"

"For one thing, Armand shot and killed Lamar tonight," Johnny said. "Seems that they had a deal to frame Morgan on this bank-robbing business and Lamar was to get five thousand dollars, but Armand wouldn't keep his word. Lamar got mad and tried for his gun, and Armand killed him. Celia says it was murder."

"It would be," Morgan said bitterly. "Armand's fast with a gun and Lamar wasn't. He had to have you looking down the barrel." He sucked in a long breath and shook his head. "Now who's going to clear me?"

"Celia," Johnny answered. "That's one thing she wants to see you about. She said to tell you she would. She didn't say how much she was in the deal with Lamar, but she's pretending it was all Armand."

"She was in it up to her neck," Morgan said. "If she was lying about that, maybe she's lying about clearing me."

"I don't think so," Johnny said. "You see, she and Armand got into a big row. She hit him, and then he really gave her one in the gut. She's hurt. I don't think she's putting on. She thinks he boogered up her insides. Doc Bridges is out of town, so she's having to grit her teeth and stand it. She says that she's going to fire Armand, so I suppose she figures she needs you to run the place. I'm guessing about that, but it seems logical. Anyhow, she said to tell you that she'll make you a reasonable deal for your part of the spread, so maybe she just wants to buy you out."

Morgan stared at Johnny as he thought about it. Lamar couldn't clear him and he still had no faith that Molly would when the time came. Maybe Celia was his only chance. Sure, Ed Smith could say he didn't believe Morgan robbed the bank, but the shadow would still be on him until he was finally and completely cleared.

"Well?" Jean said tartly. "This is what you've been looking for. You still going to be stubborn about turning yourself in?"

"No," Morgan said. "I guess it's time to see what Smith will do, but you'd better savvy one thing, Johnny. He ain't putting me in jail."

"He don't want to," Johnny said, "but we'll sure need your gun when Armand comes to town."

"You'll have it," Morgan said, "if this turns out the way you've been saying."

"I'll come down to the jail," Alcorn said. "I'm old, but I can still pull a trigger."

Johnny shook his head. "No. I don't believe you could shoot straight if you did pull a trigger. I reckon Ed would tell you that you're more important sitting in the courtroom than you are trying to play deputy."

Alcorn sat back, plainly relieved. "I guess I am at that," he said.

Morgan strode to the door. He paused to look back at Jean. "If I don't see you again. . . ."

"Don't say that!" she cried. "Don't even think it. You've got to see me again and don't you ride out of town without coming back here."

"I'll be back if Celia's telling the truth," he said. "I mean, if she does what she says she will."

"I think she will," Johnny said. "She's hurting too much to lie to you or us, or make a promise she didn't aim to keep. She thinks Armand busted up her liver when he hit her. I've got a hunch she thinks she's dying."

"She's too tough to die from getting hit in the belly," Morgan said.

He left the house and turned toward the courthouse, Johnny keeping step with him. They were silent, Morgan thinking that the old spirit of partnership with Johnny Bedlow was gone. It would be the same with Tully Bean. Too much had happened, he thought sadly, to pick up his life the way it had been when he'd left. Even if Celia meant what she had told Johnny, he could not work with her or for her.

When they reached the courthouse, Johnny said: "She's in the jail. She had to lie down and that was the only place we could put her right then."

Johnny led the way into the sheriff's office. Ed Smith stood beside his desk, anxious eyes on Morgan. He said: "I'm glad to see you, Morg. I've been hoping you'd come in."

"I'm here to see Celia," Morgan said. "If you've got a notion about jailing me. . . ."

"I don't," Ed said. "Celia's cleared you. I guess Johnny must have told you."

"He told me," Morgan said, "but I figured it might be a trap."

Ed sighed. "I'm sorry you even thought that. I'll say it again. Celia has cleared you. The law doesn't want you, but we need you as a deputy. I'll remind you that you're the reason Armand is bringing his crew into town. I figure the four of us can give him a pretty warm reception."

"That you, Morgan?" Celia called from a cell.

Ed tipped his head toward the door that opened into the cells. "Go ahead. She's been fretting about you not getting here in time."

Morgan crossed the room to the door that led into the cells. Celia lay on her back, her face contorted with pain. When she saw Morgan, she grumbled: "Took you long enough."

"I see your disposition hasn't improved much," Morgan said.

"I've got reason to have a bad disposition," she snapped. "That god-damned Buck hit me. . . ."

"Johnny told me," Morgan said. "Smith also says you've cleared me of the bank robbing frame-up."

She nodded. "But that's not the reason I sent for you. I'm getting rid of Buck. I'll divorce him as soon as I can, and I'm firing him the next time I see him. If I live and if it ever comes to court, I'll swear you had nothing to do with any bank robbery. What I wanted to see you about was the Rafter D. We've got to make a deal. . . ."

A spasm of pain knifed through her and she stopped, her face turning pale. She groaned, her lips twitching until the worst of the pain had passed. Morgan, watching her, could not doubt her agony. She had never been one to play-act about anything.

"You'll live," he said. "Just hang on till the doc gets here."

"Oh, I'll hang on," she said, "but I dunno how bad off I am." She chewed on her lower lip a moment, then she added: "You know how much I think of the spread. Nothing else means anything to me. It was the same with Pa. That's why I married Buck, and it's why I've tried to hornswoggle you out of your share. I'd still do it if I could, but I've learned one thing since Buck hit me. I can't go it alone. I've got to have a man I can trust. That's you. I'll buy you out, if you want to sell, but I want you to ramrod the outfit. Or if you want to run the ranch as partners, we'll do that."

She had been brought down a long way, he thought, to talk like this. He didn't think he'd ever hear her say she couldn't go it alone. Maybe she'd been brought to the place where she did mean it.

"All right," Morgan said. "When this is over, we'll get hold of Judge Alcorn and draw up whatever papers we need. I'm not sure it'll work, but we'll try."

"That's all I ask," she said, closing her eyes. "Just try."

XXIII

Ed Smith heard most of what was said between Morgan and his sister. Celia Armand had always been an obstinate, proud woman who had never asked anything from anybody with the exception of her father. Now she was broken. Ed wasn't sure what had broken her. It might have been the physical suffering that came from receiving Armand's blow, or it might have been the fact that her husband had struck her and walked out, forcing her to face the biggest mistake she had ever made in her life. She had never been one to admit making a mistake, but now she could not avoid it.

Morgan joined Ed, glancing at him questioningly as if asking whether Celia had meant what she'd said. Ed jerked his head toward the door. They stepped outside into the pale morning light. For a time there was only silence, the world not yet awake, then a rooster crowed and from somewhere at the other end of Main Street a dog barked.

"It ain't like Celia," Ed said. "I guess that's what you were thinking."

Morgan nodded, his expression grim. "I was saying to myself when I was coming here with Johnny that I couldn't work with Celia or for her. Now I'm not so sure. Maybe she's really changed. But then maybe, when she quits hurting, she'll be just as ornery as ever."

"Maybe," Ed said, "but I've known people who were changed because of what happened to 'em. It sure did something to Celia when Armand hit her the way he did. Not physically so much. It destroyed something in her. Pride, maybe."

"I guess you didn't hear what she said right there at the last," Morgan said. "She lowered her voice so nobody else would hear. She claims that Armand murdered Pa. You ever think of that?"

"No," Ed said, "but it's possible. He'd do anything that would get him what he wanted, and he's wanted the Rafter D as long as he's been in the country."

"She also says he'll kill her after he finishes me," Morgan went on. "He's a mad dog, Ed."

"He's that, all right," Ed agreed, "though I'm not sure all of his men are. Most of 'em are new, cowboys he's hired after your pa died. There's just two or three old hands who ain't saints, but they ain't cold-blooded killers, neither."

"Slim Turner, for instance," Morgan said.

Ed nodded. "I can think of a couple more, but three ain't enough to stop 'em, and some of the others, like the Idaho Kid, are plain poison. I figured Armand would wind up firing all the old hands, but he never got around to cleaning house. Maybe Celia wouldn't stand for it."

"He'd have to have a reason for firing them or Celia would have raised hell," Morgan agreed. "Chances are he wasn't quite ready for a showdown."

There was a moment of silence, both men thinking about what had been said, then Ed muttered: "This waiting is making my insides crawl. It's been that way most of the night. I guess I've got time to go tell Missus Lamar about Dick being killed. I should have done it sooner, but I wanted you to get here first. Tully ought to be back any minute."

"Go ahead," Morgan said. "I'll stay here."

Ed crossed the weed-covered yard to his horse, glad to be on the move even for a few minutes. The waiting was worse as the showdown came closer. He had plenty of water in the jail, and he could lock the door and put shutters on the windows and hold out all day if Armand decided to lay siege to the jail.

The prospect of defending the jail didn't worry Ed, but if

Armand chose to burn the town to force Morgan into the open, the whole game was changed. He thought of his wife and children, of the other women and children in town, and he knew he could not stay inside the jail if that happened.

A prickle of fear ran down his spine. Once he and his deputies left the safety of the jail, the odds being what they were, they'd all be killed. The other alternative was to give up Morgan and that was even more unthinkable. If Buck Armand got his way now, there would be no living with him, and Ed would be killed sooner or later. Celia could very well be right in saying that Armand had killed her father and would find a way to kill her.

He mounted and rode to the Lamar house. No light showed at any of the windows. He dismounted, tied, and walked to the front door, thinking that Molly Lamar would have stayed up all night waiting for her husband's return, if she were any other woman, but Molly was in a class by herself.

He jerked the bell pull three times, but no one answered. He pounded on the door with his fist, making enough noise, he thought, to wake the neighbors. Presently he heard someone coming. The door opened and Molly stood there, a lamp in her hand. She was, he thought, a very sleepy-looking woman, and it took her a moment to recognize him.

"Oh, it's you, Sheriff," she said in a listless voice. "Come in. I guess I don't need the lamp, do I. I didn't know it was daylight. I've been asleep."

She led the way back along the hall to her sitting room and set the lamp down. Then she turned and faced him. "Why are you here, Sheriff? If it's about that hold-up, I can tell you right now that Morgan Dill had nothing to do with it. Dick's been dipping into his safe for months to get money to gamble with, and he framed Morgan to hide the shortage of funds and make folks think Morgan took the money. He had a deal with Buck Armand so Morgan would have to leave the county."

Ed hesitated, surprised that she volunteered the information this way, information that would have ruined her husband if he were still alive. He said: "Thanks for telling me. I figured it was that way."

She sat down in a rocker, her hands fluttering uncertainly in front of her before she folded them and let them drop to her lap. "I should have told you before," she said, "but I just didn't know what to do. You see, nobody loves me any more. Dick went out to the Rafter D to get some money that Armand owed him over this deal they'd made, then he was leaving town and taking me with him." She paused and dabbed at her eyes, before she went on: "He didn't come. Morgan was here for a while. He left and didn't come back. I told him I'd clear him of the bank robbery if he . . . well, you know. . . ." Her voice trailed off.

"I understand," Ed said, knowing exactly what she meant. "Missus Lamar, I've come to give you some sad news. Your husband was shot and killed tonight by Buck Armand. It seemed that they quarreled about that money you mentioned."

"Dick's . . . dead?" She looked at him blankly, as if not believing it, then she shook her head. "That's funny, Sheriff. You know, Dick was a terrible coward. I can't imagine him having enough trouble with a man like Buck Armand to get himself killed."

"Missus Armand says it was murder," Ed said. "The body is at the undertaker's if you want to see it."

Her hands unfolded and fluttered in front of her again, and dropped back to her lap. "No, I don't want to see the body. I don't want to have anything to do with him again.

Never! Somebody else will have to arrange for the funeral. I don't know what to do."

"It will be taken care of," Ed said.

As he turned to leave the room, she said: "If you see Morgan, tell him to come and see me. He's all I've got left."

He walked out of the room. She was a strange one, he thought. She certainly wasn't grieving over Lamar's death; she didn't even act as if she were shocked by the news. Ed had a feeling she cared more about Morgan than her husband, that she had been deeply hurt by his not coming back to her, but that made very little sense, considering the way she had thrown him overboard to marry Dick Lamar. Well, there had never been very much about Molly that did make sense.

He rode back to the courthouse, the sun showing a full red circle above the eastern hills. He dismounted and tied, again pausing to listen, but he heard nothing. It was time, he thought. He walked slowly to the jail, noting that Tully stood in the doorway.

"You get everything taken care of?" Ed asked.

Tully nodded. "Funny thing, though. I didn't think the business about Lamar's bank was generally known in town, but that damned undertaker wanted to know who was going to pay him. Maybe he'd heard that the bank was robbed last night and he figured there wasn't any money left. . . ."

Ed held up a hand. He said: "Listen." The steady drumbeat of hoofs came to him. The moment was now. He said: "They're coming."

XXIV

When Morgan heard Ed Smith say they were coming, he pushed past Tully and stepped outside asking: "How do we play this, Sheriff?"

For a moment Ed didn't answer. Morgan, looking at him, saw the corners of his mouth twitch. He sensed the fear that was in the man and for an instant he thought the lawman was going to cave, but he regained control of himself.

"We play it tough," Ed said. "I'm glad the waiting's over. I thought the damned night would never end." He motioned for Morgan and Tully to go back inside. "If Armand wants to root us out of here, he's got a job to do."

He followed Morgan and Tully inside and, going to the gun rack, passed out three rifles, then kept the last one. He went to his desk, opened a drawer, took out several boxes of shells, and laid them on top of the desk. "Check your Winchesters," he said. "I think they're all loaded, but be sure. Better load your pockets with shells."

He saw that the magazine of his rifle was full, then moved to the door. He paused, glancing along the wall. He said: "Stand by the windows and let 'em have it the first shot they fire. We can put the shutters up, but we'll wait and see what they do. I just don't believe Armand's got the patience to sit it out all day with us in here."

The threat to burn the town was in all of their minds, Morgan knew. He would have considered it a bluff with any man but Buck Armand. The only way to stop him was to give himself up. If it came to that, he'd walk out with his gun blazing and end up getting killed by the Rafter D men who worked for a ranch that partly belonged to him. It couldn't end that way, he thought. It just couldn't, but if it did, he'd take Buck Armand with him.

"Give me a rifle!" Celia called. "I can shoot as good as any of you, though I don't figure it's gonna come to that. I aim to put a stop to this business when they get here."

"Stay where you are," Ed said. "It's got past the place where you can stop it."

He stepped back through the doorway and stood in front of the jail, his Winchester held at the ready. Morgan could see the riders now at the edge of town, a dust cloud rising behind them. Ed said: "If they charge us, I'm coming back in *pronto*. Tully, you slam and bar the door. I don't think they'll do that, though. Armand knows we'd cut 'em to ribbons."

The Rafter D men reached the corner of the block and stopped, Armand holding up a hand. Dust swept by them and was gone. Morgan, making a quick count, saw an even dozen. Slim Turner was in the rear of the pack. He recognized Quince Curry, but he didn't know any of the others.

"All right, Smith!" Armand yelled. "You know why we're here!"

Smith stood motionlessly, a lean, straight-backed man, the early morning sun casting his long shadow across the weed-covered yard. "Looks like you're taking an early morning ride!" he yelled back.

"Don't get smart, you jackass!" Armand shouted. "I want Morgan Dill! We're hanging him for stealing a horse from the Rafter D when he left the country in a hurry! Have you got him?"

"He's here!" Ed answered.

"Well, then, by God, send him out!" Armand bellowed. "We've been riding all night and we're tired, so let's get it over with!"

"Come and get him!" Ed said.

That jolted Armand. He snarled: "You think we can't do it?"

"It'll cost you!" Ed said. "There's four of us and we shoot damned straight, so let's see you try it!"

"We ain't gonna bust your door down," Armand said, "if that's what you're figuring on us doing! We'll give you just ten seconds to send him out! If he don't come, we're starting at the west edge of town and we'll burn one house at a time till you see the light! We don't aim to hurt nobody else, so we'll get the people out of the houses, but you'll have no town left! Now start counting or push him through the door!"

Before Ed could say a word, Celia shoved past him and walked out of the jail. She still bent forward at her waist; she still had one hand against her belly. She called: "Don't start no counting! I've got something to say to all of you!"

"Get back inside!" Armand bawled. "My God, Celia, have you lost the few brains you used to have?"

She kept walking, moving slowly as if each step hurt her. When she was halfway across the yard, she stopped. "I guess this is close enough for all of you to hear me," she said. "You boys turn around and ride back to the Rafter D. I've let this son-of-a-bitch I married run my spread too long, so I'm firing him now, and I'll divorce him as soon as I can. From now on my brother Morgan is running the outfit. Now head back. There'll be no shooting and no town burning. I'm the one who pays you and don't you forget it."

For a moment there was only a stunned silence, the men frozen in their saddles as they stared at her. Morgan, watching, admired Celia more than he ever had in his life. It took guts to walk out there as she had.

"Go on!" Celia cried impatiently. "Git!"

From somewhere in the rear of the cluster of riders a six-gun roared. Celia went back and down into the weeds of the yard. An instant later a second gun was fired and one of the riders spilled out of his saddle.

"It was the Idaho Kid!" Slim Turner yelled. "He won't shoot no more women! We didn't come here to kill our boss! I've had enough! Let's ride!"

"Me, too!" Quince Curry said.

"No, you don't!" Armand bawled. "You'll stay right here till I tell you to ride!"

It was time to sit in on the game, Morgan knew. He put his rifle down and stepped through the door, calling: "Buck, I hold you personally responsible for the murder of my sister! This is between you and me. There's no sense of anybody else getting hurt. Now, if you ain't yellow all the way through, you'll get off that horse and we'll settle this right now, just the two of us."

Armand sat hunched over the saddle horn like a great toad. This was not to his liking, Morgan sensed, not the way he had pictured it to himself, but he was cornered. If he refused, he lost status in front of his men and he would never command again.

Morgan paced toward Armand, his right hand brushing the butt of his gun, his giant shadow moving across the yard. Armand stepped down slowly, grudgingly, and started toward Morgan, his round face hard set and ugly with fury. Suddenly, as if he had lost all self-control, he began to run toward Morgan, his right hand sweeping his gun from leather.

Armand fired first, the slug kicking up dust at Morgan's feet. Morgan drew, felt the hard butt of the gun against his palm, then the kick of that gun as he pulled the trigger. Powder flame was a brilliant burst of fire in the pale morning light. The thunder of the two shots rolled through the sleeping town. Morgan stood motionlessly, waiting. He did not fire again.

Armand stopped his headlong rush as suddenly as if he had run straight into an invisible wall. His head tipped forward and he broke at knee and hip and collapsed, his gun falling from his hand. Face down in the weeds, he made one final effort to reach his gun, impelled by the driving hate he had for Morgan, but the strength was not in him. His hand fell back to the ground, his fingertips a good six inches from the handle of the gun.

Holstering his Colt, Morgan looked at the men in the street. He said: "If you boys want to go on working for Rafter D, you'd better head back to it. I'll be out later today."

For a moment they sat motionlessly as if still frozen by what had happened, then Slim Turner said: "I guess we'd better ride if we want to keep our jobs." He turned his horse and rode away. Quince Curry followed, the others slowly falling in behind them.

Ed Smith and Tully had run from the jail and were picking Celia up as Morgan turned. They carried her inside, Morgan a step behind them. They put her down on the bunk she had occupied before she ran out of the jail. If she had stayed inside, Morgan thought, she would have lived, but now she was dying and the knowledge was in her eyes as she turned them to Morgan's face. She held up a hand and he took it.

Strange, he thought, that she had hated him and fought him most of his life, yet now, with death only seconds away, she reached for his hand. He should say something, but he didn't know what to say that would make any sense at a time like this. He could not bring himself to lie and tell her she was going to be all right.

"Is that bastard of a husband of mine dead?" she asked.

"He's dead," Morgan answered.

"Good," she said, her voice so low Morgan could barely hear what she said. "I'll soon be seeing him in hell." Blood

217

bubbled at the corners of her mouth in a crimson froth. "It's yours without no more trouble, Morgan, the whole damned layout. Make it a good spread like Pa did." She stopped and Morgan thought she was gone, but a moment later she added: "Funny how it started out, ain't it? All of my scheming didn't get me nowhere."

A moment later she was dead. He turned and walked out into the morning sunlight. It was indeed funny, he thought. He wasn't sure what had prompted Celia to run out of the jail unless she had been determined to show the crew that she was the boss, to get the best of Buck Armand in front of the men who were important to both of them. One thing was plain. It was her death that had made possible the duel between him and Armand, shocking the men into immobility. If Morgan had walked out of the jail before Celia made her appearance, he would have been cut down by a dozen slugs, and so, regardless of her intentions, his sister had saved his life.

He moved slowly along deserted Main Street, knowing that he had much to do. One thing was essential, to give everyone in the county a different image of the Rafter D than they'd had through the past years. It would still be the biggest and most powerful ranch in the county, but the power would be used in a different way than it had been in the past.

He did not see Jean Runyan come around the corner until she was within a few feet of him. Then he heard her cry out in a nearly hysterical voice: "Are you all right, Morgan? I heard the shooting. The judge didn't want me to come, but I had to. Are you all right?"

"Of course, I'm all right," he said as he took her into his arms. "The judge was right. If there had been a big fight, it wouldn't have been safe for you to be on the street."

She buried her face against his shirt and began to cry.

218

He asked: "What are you crying about? I just told you I was all right."

She said, her voice muffled: "I'm crying because I'm so happy that you're still alive."

"Now that's a good reason to cry, ain't it?" he asked. "I'd better warn you about something now that the trouble is over. I'm aiming to court you, and then I'm going to marry you."

She tipped her head back and smiled up at him. "Can't we just skip the courting and get married? I loved you when I was a little girl, but you didn't have eyes for anyone but Molly. I don't want to wait. I don't want to wait at all."

He laughed softly and kissed her. "Why, when you get right down to it, I don't want to wait, either."

About the Author

Wayne D. Overholser won three Spur Awards from the Western Writers of America and has a long list of fine Western titles to his credit. He was born in Pomeroy, Washington, and attended the University of Montana, University of Oregon, and the University of Southern California before becoming a public schoolteacher and principal in various Oregon communities. He began writing for Western pulp magazines in 1936 and within a couple of years was a regular contributor to Street & Smith's *Western Story Magazine* and Fiction House's *Lariat Story Magazine*. *Buckaroo's Code* (1947) was his first Western novel and remains one of his best. In the 1950s and 1960s, having retired from academic work to concentrate on writing, he would publish as many as four books a year under his own name or a pseudonym, most prominently as Joseph Wayne. *The Violent Land* (1954), *The Lone Deputy* (1957), *The Bitter Night* (1961), and *Riders of the Sundowns* (1997) are among the finest of the Overholser titles. *The Sweet and Bitter Land* (1950), *Bunch Grass* (1955), and *Land of Promises* (1962) are among the best Joseph Wayne titles, and *Law Man* (1953) is a most rewarding novel under the Lee Leighton pseudonym. Overholser's Western novels, whatever the byline, are based on a solid knowledge of the history and customs of the 19th-Century West, particularly when set in his two favorite Western states, Oregon and Colorado. Many of his novels are first-person narratives, a technique that tends to bring an added dimension of vividness to the frontier experiences of his narrators and frequently, as in *Cast a Long Shadow* (1957), the female characters one encounters are among the most memorable. He wrote his numerous novels with a consistent skill and an uncommon sensitivity to the depths of human character. Almost invariably, his stories weave a spell of their own with their scenes and images of social and economic forces often in conflict and the diverse ways of life and personalities that made the American Western frontier so unique a time and place in human history. *Bitter Wind* will be his next **Five Star Western**.